Coexistence

COEXISTENCE

STORIES

Billy-Ray Belcourt

W. W. NORTON & COMPANY
Independent Publishers Since 1923

For information about permission to reproduce selections from
this book, write to Permissions, W. W. Norton & Company, Inc.,
500 Fifth Avenue, New York, NY 10110

For information about special discounts for bulk purchases,
please contact W. W. Norton Special Sales at
specialsales@wwnorton.com or 800-233-4830

Manufacturing by Lake Book Manufacturing
Book design by Brooke Koven
Production manager: Louise Mattarelliano

ISBN 978-1-324-07594-3 (pbk)

W. W. Norton & Company, Inc.
500 Fifth Avenue, New York, N.Y. 10110
www.wwnorton.com

W. W. Norton & Company Ltd.
15 Carlisle Street, London W1D 3BS

1 2 3 4 5 6 7 8 9 0

CONTENTS

Coexistence

One Woman's Memories

THERE ARE THREE PORTRAITS of Jesus in Louise's home. In all of them, Jesus' gaze is both sincere and unspecific; it evokes whatever the onlooker needs it to but always with deep seriousness. Today, his gaze reflects Louise's somberness. Because it feels good to have one's emotions acknowledged without judgment, she hasn't taken down the portraits. Jesus represents for her a force in the world that nourishes, like motherhood. To be a mother is to represent for someone else life as an abstract quality.

Louise isn't a practicing Catholic, but she does believe in heaven and in suffering's transmutability. Louise might say that suffering doesn't exist for the sake of itself—people suffer in order to keep living, to figure out how to live differently. She wouldn't use the word "suffering," however; she would name it something more identifiable, like a headache or fatigue or joint pain or, more ambiguously, "the past." Louise tends to treat the past with ambivalence, as if it were an empty house she wanders through but won't drag furniture inside of. And yet the walls of her home are cluttered with photographs of her parents and siblings and late husband but especially her son, Paul, tracing his childhood to the near present.

A photograph represents the past without bringing it to life. A photograph gives shape to history; it allows us to fashion a landscape of feeling, suppressing whatever other emotional detail is ungovernable. A photograph is a ladder that goes backward in time, a ladder we can push away whenever we want. With photographs, we can obscure the past as much as illuminate it.

This afternoon the house is silent and cold. Louise sits on a floral-patterned couch beside a telephone, its receiver gray and hard and unattractive in the way all new technology seems ugly to her. When she dials Paul, she doesn't have to think about his number; it exists inside her like a heartbeat. Every time they speak, she's struck by how close his voice sounds, as though he's across a room and not hundreds of miles away. As the phone rings, Louise considers leaving a voicemail but decides against it. She hangs up and looks over at Jesus again.

It is winter and she is lonely. The past swells around her in all its glistening clarity.

Against her nature, she wants to discuss, with Paul, the events of her life. It's a new urge. She has lived through so much and yet has discussed so little about that living. A new century has begun, and she still feels like a part of the preceding one. She belongs to the twentieth century, is indivisible from it. However long she lives, however greatly the world changes, that fact remains.

People don't really expire, Louise thinks. People die, but even in death they continue aging in crooked photographs along a wall in someone's house.

What does it mean to be a living monument? The question hovers around her all night.

• • •

IT's THE MIDDLE OF FEBRUARY in the subarctic. Snow has fallen over everything indiscriminately. The aspens around the reserve lost their leaves months ago. Now their branches jut out frailly toward the sky, as though in prayer. The blue is so expansive it's unreal, the opposite of human consciousness. Louise is shoveling snow off the path that leads to her car, which has been idling to melt the ice covering the windshield. She wipes sweat from her forehead and looks at the forest; it elicits sympathy, not the cruel kind, but rather something akin to closeness. She identifies in both the forest and in herself a state of wavering. She too has endured season after season of loss. Without foliage, the trees don't tremble. This morning, it's Louise who does. It's as if the winter she is currently living through has embedded itself inside her. Does she have a use for her sadness, which feels so much like winter? Yes, because it's also a homeland, a place where she is never in exile.

The drive to the grocery store can take twice as long in snowy conditions. Louise moves slowly along the icy highway. The car has gone mostly unattended to since her husband's death. They were never officially married, though she thinks of him as her husband all the same. In Louise's mind, marriage is for the young. When they met, he was a non-status Indian because his mother had married a non-status man and in so doing surrendered Indian status—this gender-biased clause in the Indian Act wouldn't get amended for several more decades; status Indian men had the power to transmit status, but Indian women could only have theirs taken away; because of who they loved they could cease to be Indian in the eyes of the government. Louise's mother advised them not to marry. It was Indian common sense. When Paul was born, they gave him Louise's surname. Minor manipulations of colonial law shaped family life. When her husband's Indian status was at last restored, in the late eighties, it was too late. By then it seemed silly to have their love, which was already so instilled with truth, codified by the government.

She pulls into the town where she does her shopping, in what some historians call a "railway town," one that came into being as the railway etched itself into the prairies like a tear. For decades, a de facto mode of segregation was in place. The town was ruled by white families tied first to homesteading then to the railway and then later to lumbering. Indigenous peoples came and went, because colonization meant that they were implicated in the settler economy, but they rarely lingered. Horror stories abounded. People kept away. Louise is a part of this history, as are her loved ones, though she has never thought to describe it as racist. To her, it was simply the way things were, which is, of course, a function of racism.

In the grocery store, Louise puts more into her cart than she needs. Some white people stare at her rudely, but she doesn't notice. She runs into a distant cousin in the produce aisle, and they catch up for a few minutes. She desires a fuller conversation, but their location runs counter to that desire. It's as if everyone is listening in. She promises to stop by the cousin's place later in the week. When she gets back into her car, it's frigid again. She blows into her hands and blasts the heat while a song she's never heard before plays on the radio.

Louise drives even more slowly on the way back to the reserve under heavy snowfall. At one point she pulls onto a dirt road and puts the hazard lights on, closes her eyes, and rests her head against the steering wheel. The heat cascades over her face. She remains this way for a long time.

AT HOME, LOUISE CHECKS to see if she's missed any calls. She hasn't. She'll have to wait until evening to call Paul again, when he returns home from work. He lives in Edmonton and is the first in her family to have earned a post-secondary degree. When he convocated, Louise sobbed in her seat in the grand auditorium. The ceremony marked for her a subtle break from history. Paul would live a better life. It was a thought undercut with a generation's hope. As Paul put down roots in the city, built his better life down south, and fell in love with a Cree woman from a nearby reserve, he grew distant from his parents, from his childhood North. Louise wonders how it is that a mother and son cleave apart; it betrays what she knows about being a person. The cleaving was so gradual and mysterious it was almost as if it were an inevitability. Her son turned inscrutable. Her grief over this feels so private that she doesn't give it outward expression, which only adds to the air of disconnection between them. Does she wish she had had more children? Sometimes. Mostly, though, she wants to undo time or to live the same life over again. To make small adjustments that would, of course, change everything.

She looks at the photographs on her wall, pausing on the older ones of her father. He was a quiet man; his imposing stature was its own statement, and so his body spoke for him. His long silences accrued into an entire life. Born years before any of the towns formed along the lake, he predated the railway but came after a Catholic missionary presence. He had memories of the signing of Treaty 8, an agreement that his elders assumed was meant to ensure communal living, as well as nightmares about being unable to leave the reserve without the permission of the Indian agent, but he never spoke about them to Louise. He didn't talk much about himself. Not many of his generation did. They lived through land loss and famine and the inception of the residential school system. They were the first cohort of parents who had to endure the seizure of their children in the name of state-mandated colonial education. Louise thinks about the reserve today and shudders at the thought of it suddenly emptied of children. A place without children has no future. Her father had to live out this terrible reality. Amid this living nightmare, he considered enlisting in the Canadian army to fight in Europe. He would've had to get enfranchised, to give up Indian status. Some native men were doing so with the dream of escaping the violence of colonization. Her father knew this dream was an impossible one. Europe would only plunge them into a different violence and spit them back into the old one if they survived. He had to defend his own children, his own people, he decided.

They'd lived on the same expanse of land until he died from heart disease. Louise used to say that he died of a broken heart. The metaphor consoled her. The heart was the first of his organs to falter under the pressures of the long twentieth century. Louise thinks about him all the time. She felt close to him her whole life. He helped build the house she lives in now. Sometimes she touches the walls as though to do so is to touch him. It's an act of mourning. More than that, it's how she collapses the past into the present. It's a way of staying alive.

.   .   .

LATER, LOUISE AT LAST gets Paul on the phone. After they exchange pleasantries, Louise tells him she'd like to discuss her life. She doesn't want to ignore the urge or allow it to dissipate. She is already tired of waiting.

6

"What do you mean? Did something happen?" he asks.

"No, no, nothing happened." She laughs gently. "I want to talk to you about my past."

It's a foreign sentence. Neither has heard the other utter it before. It occurs to Paul that he knows very little about his mother's past. What he knows is limited to images, brief anecdotes, old family jokes. He feels a pang of shame about this state of unknowing.

If a mother is a shape of unknowing, then a son is a bit of dying light.

"I'm listening, Mom. You have my undivided attention."

Louise laughs again, nervously this time, unsure where or how to start. She fidgets with the phone cord.

"The summer after my last year at the mission," she says finally.

Paul hasn't heard that word in a while—*mission*. It's the colloquial way people refer to one of the residential schools that was on the shores of the lake. The government forced Louise to attend one for the entirety of her primary and secondary schooling. Some years she wasn't allowed to leave the property. Other years, luckier ones (what is luck in the face of genocide?), she could visit family on weekends and during the summer. The fact that it was never clear when she'd be able to leave was its own torture. Louise has never said much about her time there, nor will she go into much detail tonight. Lately, her mind has turned to the memory of Sue, a girl she befriended as a teen. They were inseparable. What they had was more than friendship; each represented for the other a life reminiscent of their rez upbringings, of early childhoods suffused with joy. For many years, they were a duo before they were individuals.

"Sue and I vowed to go on an adventure right after we left the mission," she said. "It was all we talked about. It saved us, in a way. We were going to cross the valley to the north, maybe even follow the river back to the mountains in the west. Most of that was dreaming, naturally. What ended up happening was we'd meet halfway between our reserves and find the water from there. We'd sit in the lake and talk about the world as though it was owed to us."

"Whereabouts?" Paul asks, partly so that Louise feels listened to, partly because the newness of the memory makes her feel like a stranger to him.

Louise can't remember. "Somewhere secluded, somewhere no one would find us," she explains.

"The love I felt for her was stronger than I'd ever experienced. We held hands sometimes, and something in me ached when we did. I didn't know that two Cree girls could fall in love. I didn't think to ask Sue if she loved me. That possibility was absurd, really. We were still healing from the school, but we tried to live as though we were free all the same. We spent our summers that way until I met your father."

Paul hadn't heard Louise talk about Sue before, for she wasn't prone to bouts of nostalgia. To hear Louise speak about her as an object of unrequited love moves him. He thinks about his own lost loves, but none of them warrant the awe he detects in Louise's voice. He's reminded that there are plenty of things he doesn't know about his mother.

"Do you still talk to her?"

"We lost touch sometime in the eighties. We wrote letters back then. Simple dispatches about our lives. They didn't seem special at the time, but I sift through them nowadays and feel emotional. In one of them, she told me about her children, all ten of them. Her family must be huge, getting bigger and bigger every year."

Paul winces at the tinge of melancholy in this remark. He

thinks about how absent he's been, about how alienating his distance must be. Why has he stayed away? He isn't entirely certain. Life on the reserve feels too overdetermined, its scripts seemingly already written. In the city, Paul found that he could begin in his mind and create different rules, comport himself however he wanted. Existing in history's aftermath, of course, isn't ever that simple, but sometimes to change our circumstances of living we have to pretend that's the case. We all have it in ourselves to be self-deceiving. Nothing in him explicitly yearns for northern Alberta, a difficult truth to hold. Sometimes he feels that this is a personal failing. Worse, a social one. When he's especially loathsome, he feels that he's failed to be a good son as well as a good native. Visiting the reserve is a duty he's happy to carry out, all the same; he enjoys spending time with Louise. But it's in the city that he's most at peace.

"Did you ever talk to Dad about Sue?" Paul asks plainly. He isn't sure how sentimental to be about the conversation.

Louise thinks. She can hear Paul's breathing, his soft inhalations.

"Your father was as heterosexual as can be."

They laugh. Paul thinks the same could be said about him. Maybe it's an inherited defect.

"My attraction to him never wavered," Louise continues, "so I didn't think too much about it, to be honest. I thought he was the most handsome man on the reserve."

She glances at a black-and-white photo of him. He's wearing denim and a cowboy hat and giving off an aura of goodness. She still feels good by extension.

"When I had you, when we moved into this house, I knew I didn't need anything else. I knew I'd be happy for a long time."

Something suddenly feels heavy in both Louise and Paul. The subject of her husband, his father, hadn't come up since the funeral in the fall. He died of a heart attack in the night (a family of natives with bad hearts isn't uncommon). Louise woke and he didn't. She always thought that she'd depart first. His death fractured her reality, made her feel lopsided and blurry. They were both overtaken by the blurriness of grief, just not in the same place. To grieve apart from one another is itself a tragedy.

"When he died," Louise went on, her voice breaking, "I had to figure out how to keep living. I did everything with him. We never slept in different beds, not once. We were together for so long and yet I still wanted more time."

Some people don't take to the singular *I*.

Paul thinks about his father. He was loud and energetic, and he loved fishing and gardening. Paul remembers waking up at dawn to head out onto the lake in their small boat; on the water, his father told him stories about fish as well as the ways Cree people have related to the moose and the deer as kin since time immemorial, which was his way of passing down ancestral knowledge. Paul regrets having missed out on so many of his last days. No one knew they were his last, but Paul wasn't around anyways. He doesn't talk to the dead. It doesn't come naturally to him. He wishes someone had taught him how. Instead, he's listening to his mother on the phone, picturing her small body, which he hasn't seen in person since Christmas. For the sake of the holiday, they didn't talk about the past or the dead. Perhaps they should have. That task is always more urgent than anything else. Maybe it's all they can do now.

"I suppose what I'm saying is that I miss him so much," Louise says.

"I miss him too, Mom."

Silence. Wind rustles outside both of their windows. It's expected to be one of the coldest nights of the year.

"Maybe you could come stay with me for a while," Paul says.

"We've got plenty of space. I can come pick you up as soon as this weekend."

Louise looks out the window and sees that the snowy field across the road is shimmering. There are many weeks of winter ahead, but at least the earth can still shimmer.

Louise's sense of self is tied to her home. She can't leave the reserve. All her memories are here. Gratitude swells in her as she realizes this.

"I'll think about it, dear," she says.

"OK, Mom, I'll call you tomorrow, how's that?"

"I'd like that," she says.

· · ·

IN BED, LOUISE'S BODY feels heavy with the day's proceedings. Then, for a moment, she swears she can smell her husband. His aroma swirls around her once again—soil, sweat, a hint of gasoline. It fades as quickly as it emerged, but she understands at last that he hasn't left her entirely.

Sometimes to remember is enough, she thinks, then she says it out loud.

Lived Experience

THE AIR IS SO HUMID and heavy that my small non-airconditioned studio feels like a sick joke. I'm sitting on an old family couch in too-big underwear because I haven't eaten anything but fruit and cereal in weeks. The apartment, located just off the river valley, is mostly empty, save for the couch, a mattress on the floor, a box TV, and a print of Picasso's *Woman with Bangs* stationed in the bathroom, all of which I either inherited or stole. The walls are so thin that I often hear my neighbors fucking, which makes me feel both more and less a part of the world. Their animal sounds remind me that the solitary *I* is a trick of the light and that the plural is dense and unbearable.

Tonight I've been messaging with a deluge of men on various hookup apps. "Deluge" because nothing about it is graceful or subtle. I relinquish my sense of self every time I log on. I use language like an unsentimental tool, something depersonalized and brutish. When I'm horny I'm a small frenzy, more weather than person.

Some men want to kill me more than they want to sleep with me. Someone says he wants to fuck me, but only if I'm under a blanket, ass out. Another man blocks me when I tell him I'm native. The majority are wasting time, keeping themselves busy and at a distance from their lonely lives. I'm lonely too, but not in a way that can be cured by sexting. If anything, the sexting exacerbates the feeling that no one can satisfy my romantic desires. Eventually, a man whose username is a car emoji tells me he's in the area and is willing to park on the street outside my building for a quick blow job. Because I'm bored, I tell him I can be ready in ten minutes. I put on shorts and a T-shirt and swat dandruff out of my hair.

My phone says he's twenty feet away. I see his car first, which is very clean, as if it just went through the wash. Maybe he wants to be pure, I think, knowing our rendezvous is antithetical to that noble desire. I laugh a little; nothing I've done has ever felt noble. My car is always cluttered with empty water bottles and fast food wrappers, always on the verge of running out of gas.

He's parked just outside the glow of a streetlight. Blue light from the dashboard disappears his face. I try to focus my eyes to see him clearly, but he looks more like a digital image than a human. My heart thuds in my chest. There's still time to turn around, but I don't.

He's parked on a slope, so when I pull myself into the passenger seat I feel as though I'm falling. I grab on to the dash to steady myself, then I look him squarely in the face. He's older than I expected. His graying hair is neatly sculpted, and his thick-rimmed glasses look expensive and thoughtfully selected. He's dressed smartly, in a pullover and chinos. He reminds me of my English professors. We are opposites. My shorts have a hole at the waistline and my T-shirt is one I've had since high school. I don't remember the last time I washed either of them. What I feel for him isn't inexplicable or vague. It's precise: I'm not attracted to him. Nothing about my internal climate suggests I want to touch his genitals. It occurs to me that he never asked my age.

"Tom?" he asks. I regret having told him my name. I nod.

"I'm Grant. You're hot," he says nervously. I'm neither hot nor unattractive; I understand what he means is that I'm not a concept, which is to say I'm available to him. I'm an object in the world among other objects. He can reach out and take me.

"Thanks."

"So, you're into older men?"

The question bears its own kind of light. It brings something that was hidden into focus. I wonder if he expects a story of violation or abandonment from me, whether that's part of my erotic possibility. At the same time, the question dispels the mystery that a hookup of this sort requires for me—it implies biographical detail, it reveals too much about the person he is, which is unsexy. Still, I answer him.

"I suppose so, but I'm into all kinds of men."

Just then someone walks by, peers in and smiles at me. Maybe he heard what I said through the slight opening in the window. I catch a glimpse of his face and notice he's more classically attractive than Grant. I wish I were with him instead.

I see that Grant is rubbing his crotch and realize he doesn't care who I am or what I want. He interprets my glance as consent, unzips his pants and pulls out his dick. By now, it seems easier to comply than it does to leave. I wonder if this is a flaw in my brain chemistry, or a consequence of youth. When I'm older, when my frontal lobe is fully developed, I'll think and act differently. I repeat this in my head as I would a small prayer.

He presses two fingers against the base of his dick, making it as erect as possible, then he nods toward it. A simple cue. Instinctively, I close my eyes and open my mouth. I bend toward him, arching over the middle console. I must look like a question mark.

When he drives away, my mouth is raw, achy. I assess each streetlight one by one. Most flicker; a few are burnt out.

I open the app and see our faces side by side on the grid. I block him.

Shame is a flickering streetlight in the middle of the night.

Shame has turned me into a flickering man in the middle of my own life.

I GARGLE MOUTHWASH in front of the bathroom mirror. What do I see? A man. Some nights to be a man is to be a lost cause. In that story, no one ends up happy. What did I get from this encounter? A strange memory, a bad taste in my mouth.

I shouldn't treat my body like a shore for others to shipwreck onto. Somehow no one has told me this yet.

I first downloaded the app a year ago. I avoided it as if it were a perversity, though I was really just afraid of my own longings. I hooked up with the first man who messaged me. My hands trembled the entire time. He told me I looked like I was going to cry, but that didn't stop him. I think about this all the time. Too many nights have looked the same: a man and a man in a car or a bedroom, one or both failing to tell the truth. What did I want from these men? A little miracle, something new.

Maybe I've asked for too much. I vow then to delete the app; I won't let men ruin me.

IN THE FALL, after having sworn off men, I meet Will in a twentieth-century history class. I sit beside him because he's also Cree. When he tells me he's a painter, I swoon, because I believe that art is a kind of grace. Some things seem inherently pure, to make the world purer by virtue of their existence. To paint the world is to believe in it. What do I believe in? The inevitability of life. My only job is to stay alive. Will's job is to stay alive too, but he also has to look at the world and not flinch. He has to look at the world and render it anew on a blank canvas.

During an icebreaker, I learn that he's from a reserve in the northeast and is in the final semester of a fine arts degree. He works with watercolors because they transcend their context—they bleed. In this way, he tells me, their beauty is implicit. He's applied to graduate programs across the country, not because he thinks he needs to hone his technique, but because the funding is decent and he'd rather be in a classroom than selling his labor elsewhere. I tell him I'm from a reserve in the northwest, probably four hours from his (as the crow flies).

"And why the interest in the twentieth century?" he asks.

"We're all citizens of the twentieth century," I say, as if the line had been rehearsed, though this was the first time I'd put that idea into words. "Especially natives. I don't think it ever ended for us."

He nods somberly. "Last term, I painted a series of portraits based on photographs I found of native people in the nineties. I suppose, in a way, I was subconsciously acting out that historical debt . . . Is that Indian time?"

We laugh. In academia, jokes about the native condition are rare. My armor weakens. Will asks what I do in my spare time. "It can't all be philosophical quips," he adds, smirking.

Before I can answer, the instructor calls the class back to order.

. . .

ON OUR FIRST DATE, we get coffee and walk through the river valley. It's September, so the trees are still green and the sun is so gentle it makes me feel whole and human. Will leads me to a bench where he goes to sketch when he wants to reset his mind. It's not far from a densely forested spot where men sometimes cruise at night.

Washed in yellow, his face looks different, but beautiful still. I feel beautiful because he's looking at me. Is that what beauty is—a relation of proximity, a shared subjectivity?

"I thought about asking if I could draw you," he says into the sunlight, squinting.

I want to study him too. His hair is messy and long; it falls over his face as he speaks. His eyebrows are thick hyphens. He's tall, broad-shouldered. His right leg shakes even when he's sitting still. The total effect is that he seems to cleave into negative space, to subjugate it. I read somewhere that before colonization Crees were the tallest people on Earth. What are we now?

"What are you thinking about?"

"The sky, the trees, our hands," I say, mostly unseriously, but he reaches for my hand anyways as though I'd invited him to do so. He encases it in both of his, which are long and calloused, the hands of someone who makes things.

What have I made? Some mistakes, something almost in the shape of a life.

In the distance, I hear vehicles traversing a bridge. I look over and glimpse the newly constructed suicide barriers. In a single living moment all of the world's beauty and terror can coexist.

Will says, "I would like to lie in the grass."

He springs off the bench and onto the field in front of us. He looks at me inquisitively. I lie down beside him and look up at the clouds, at all the fragmented blue. The pleasure of looking at what he's looking at almost overwhelms me.

We stay like this for an hour. Our bodies brush, but only briefly. Birds chatter around us, families with small children come and go. It seems that Will himself—and not just his art—emits an aura of purity. It's not something I can see or measure. But it makes everything around him somehow less polluted and undignified, including me.

•   •   •

IN HISTORY CLASS, we study the world wars. Then we narrow our focus on Canada. We don't examine colonialism as the long, costly war that it was and still is. Indigenous struggles for life and land are barely alluded to, let alone all the state-sanctioned atrocities of the twentieth century. I sit still until I'm tired of feeling like a ghost. Then I raise my hand.

"Respectfully," I say, "I'm curious if we'll discuss Indigenous nations or colonialism at all?"

The instructor, a good-looking man in a too-big blazer, lifts a hand to his face, then rubs his chin.

"Honestly," he says, "I don't have the training to do it justice. I wouldn't want to get anything wrong. I know some of my colleagues study the topic, so hopefully a future class will satisfy your curiosity."

If I speak, my voice will waver. The instructor's remarks are an existential blow. In a way, the elision reaffirms how ungrievable Indigenous suffering is in the course's conceptual frame. My body protests, I'm shaking. Will sees that I'm rattled and presses his leg against mine, then rests his head on my shoulder. I take in the aroma of his shampoo—pomegranate. We are together in our minor grief. That he exists, that he and I constitute a "we," however budding and unstable, is enough of a counter, today, to historical ignorance. We aren't overdetermined by the instructor's politics of forgetting.

As the lecture continues, Will doesn't move, his head remains on my shoulder. It's a gesture so caring I almost can't stand it.

. . .

A NEW RHYTHM between us takes shape: after class we take the train over the river to my place. When we arrive, when we sit on the floor or lie on the mattress, I analyze his body language and facial expressions for signs that he's losing interest. That I find none feels like a blessing. One night I cook tomato and macarrassed that it's the only dish I know how to make. Will reminds me that we ate the same meals as kids; the small worlds we come from resemble each other. The soup, however simple and humble, is an homage to our moms, our kokums. I suggest to Will that the soup is "a transmission of maternal knowledge" and he laughs, kisses me on the forehead and neck.

"Always philosophizing."

To be thought of this way delights me. No one has ever described my thinking as philosophical.

We spend whole evenings together in bed, shirtless and needy.

Then, we have sex for the first time. We forget to close the blinds completely, so streetlight falls on us in pieces. I avoided getting naked during hookups, not wanting to expose myself entirely, but now nakedness feels necessary—we aren't trying to hide our true selves. After undressing, Will and I embrace. I taste his sweat, and its sweetness fills me up like an emotion.

It's October, and the shorter days have made us hungrier, depriving us of light and forcing us to look for it in other people.

We grind into each other. I think about a river crashing against the riverbanks, about how euphoric it is to exceed your outer limits.

Two pairs of hands, two mouths, two dicks—the math is easy for once. Thank god, I keep thinking, thank god.

I don't bottom much, mostly because I haven't felt the desire to do so with anyone I met from the app, but now the desire is evident. I hand Will a condom and he rolls it onto himself methodically. He pushes softly into me, radiating warmth. I feel safe and eager and happy. I love the simplicity of these feelings, I'm thankful for them. Two young men, one moving inside the other. It's all so easy and perfect.

"You're really beautiful," Will says, then he says it again. The more he says it the more I believe it.

We come at the same time. We continue kissing; he continues fucking me.

I don't want to stop. I want to start over and experience it again. There isn't much more I would need to have a good life. Is that wishful thinking? Who cares.

Will eventually falls asleep on my chest, and I run my hand through his hair. I resist tiredness. I want to extend the day for as long as I can. To sleep feels like a betrayal of living. So, I close my eyes and try to remember everything, which is also called dreaming.

≣

WILL INVITES ME to Thanksgiving at his reserve. We're on the highway in his pickup truck and we're listening to country music and we're in love.

At first, the landscape is mostly fields of canola. A landscape conceals as much as it makes visible. It seems straightforward, something we should all agree on. A farmer's field is a story of dispossession; there are those who take and those who are taken from. I'm waiting for everyone else to admit this.

Soon the topography changes, and we're surrounded by trees.

"Did you know the boreal forest is the largest forest in the world?" Will asks.

"I had no idea, somehow."

"It wraps right around the northern hemisphere. We need it to breathe."

I let his comment hang in the air. What else wraps around the northern hemisphere? History, its many wounded.

• • •

WILL'S MOM'S HOUSE is at the end of a long and winding dirt road. It looks like every house on every reserve: two stories, blue siding, a roof in slight disrepair, a large living room window, a blanket with several howling wolves woven into it draped over the window, an unfinished basement. She hugs us both as soon as we step inside. Her hair is shaped in a firm bob and she's wearing denim on denim, a sartorial tradition that's more Cree than it is Canadian, in my opinion. Her face is symmetrical and pretty and, like Will, she exudes compassion. She has a kind of gravity, something I feel pulled into, but not unwillingly.

"You're so skinny," she says. "I can't wait to feed you."

The smell of meat and gravy and frybread fills the house. I

think about my family, my mom. One day I'll bring Will to my reserve too, I decide. I owe them a visit. In showing him my little corner of the boreal forest, I'll show him my past, which is one of the most intimate acts available to anyone. I understand that he's extending a precious vulnerability toward me.

We sit at the kitchen table with his mom, two aunts, two uncles, and a kokum. About a dozen kids, all under eighteen, are scattered throughout the house. Laughter wells up from every room. I want to watch Will interact with his relatives more than I feel the need to contribute to the conversation. His mom notices my quietness.

"So, has Will told you how I found out he was gay?" she asks.

Will's face reddens. "Don't do this," he says timidly. Everyone laughs.

"No, he hasn't," I say, happy to be a co-conspirator in his minor embarrassment.

She sits up straighter. "Well, he was in high school," she begins. "I woke up in the middle of the night to use the washroom and found him watching gay porn on the computer. I couldn't decipher what it was at first, until the quiet noises became clearer. I'll never forget how petrified he looked when he turned around and saw me. I laughed until I cried."

"That's not normal, by the way," Will chimes in. "Normal parents don't do that." There's a tenderness underneath his performed awkwardness, her ribbing.

"We still had dial-up internet!" she adds. "I don't know why he was trying to watch porn on that old ass computer. It would've been easier to just close his eyes and imagine it!" At this, his aunts and uncles become hysterical.

We aren't lonely people, at least not today.

Will's mom goes on as the laughter subsides, "We love him very much and we will love whoever he brings home." She reaches for my hand, and I open it for her the way the October day seemed to open up specifically for us, a handful of Crees on a small rez in northern Alberta. What do you a call a handful of Crees? A laughter.

After something else fixes the group's attention, Will leans over and kisses me on the lips, longer than I expect given the relatives around us. I'm anxious at first, then I surrender to the gesture, relaxing, for the first time, into the publicness of our queer Cree joy.

ON THE DRIVE BACK to the city, I think about how in the years since coming out I mistook lust for something grander. Before Will, men treated me like a museum artifact to pick up, then put back down or walk away from. I'd been as engrossing as humidity and hadn't noticed. Now I didn't want to long and ache for nothing. Something inside me, it seems, is opening like a door, and maybe Will is already wherever that door leads to. That's what love is—someone else's spirit moving through you. When someone moves through you they leave behind a small trace of human life. It's how we know we're still alive.

"Tell me about your mom," I say as we round a bend and the city comes into view like a sudden moon.

"She believes in kindness and the afterlife, in redemption," Will says.

"Is she spiritual?"

"I think it has more to do with her upbringing, how much loss she went through. She lost her dad at a young age, and then my dad died when I was young."

I rest my hand on his thigh. Somehow it hadn't come up before.

"He was attacked in the city one summer, while running an errand. My mom pleaded to the cops that it was racially motivated but they didn't listen to her. They said it was because he was in the wrong place at the wrong time."

"Fuck."

"We're still being hunted," he says. It's a remark we both have trouble doing anything with. It's too honest. Being Indigenous in the twenty-first century means that a single hour can be governed simultaneously by joy and sadness. If sadness could fill up a truck we'd be drowning right now, but that's only part of the story. We still believe in the future, so we keep surviving to live in it.

"What was he like—your dad?"

"Sweet, super loving, not a toxic bone in him. He taught me so much simply by being gentle to others," Will says. "My mom talks to him every night. I do sometimes too. I've drawn him dozens of times. I suppose that's my particular spiritual practice. I really do believe that to draw someone is to reach out to them."

≡

THEN IT'S NOVEMBER, a time for self-reflection.

It takes all my restraint not to fixate on an eventual uncoupling, even though Will's desire for me hasn't waned. I scan his Twitter and Instagram profiles for some hidden truth, but all I learn is that he too is a person in the world. It's so easy to invent the conditions of one's demise, just like a forest does when winter encroaches. I love the trees, but I decide I don't want to be like them. Why does anyone stay with anyone else? Routine, fate, senselessness, true love. These seem like the only options.

After a long day of class and studio work, Will comes over, and I wilt a little when he pulls me into his chest.

"What's wrong?" Will asks.

"Maybe it's because I'm broke as fuck and have tons of looming deadlines, but my mind's been racing today. I can't sit still or concentrate on anything," I say.

"Same, I'm going to have to hustle to be ready for the thesis exhibit. I thought about pulling an all-nighter at the studio tonight, to be honest. I wanted to be with you, though," he says. "Now, when I picture my day I picture you in it."

I want to sob, but I don't want to add to my air of psychic instability. Instead I say, "That's literally the nicest thing anyone's ever said to me."

After midnight, we decide to have a bath. My tub is shallow and narrow, but we manage to fit both our bodies in it. Candles flicker on flat surfaces around us, throwing small shadows everywhere. Two mostly empty shampoo bottles teeter in a corner. We don't need to say anything; we are tired and in love. I want to spend the whole night this way, but that would be impractical, as so much about love is. To be in a bathtub with another man feels like more than I deserve. I feel satisfied with the scale of my living, the small contours of my existence.

≡

WILL'S THESIS EXHIBIT falls on a cold December day. I haven't seen him much over the last few days, as he's been working nonstop. I managed to hold off some of my separation anxiety, concentrating on coursework, but by the day of his show my solitude feels rotten. I promised I would meet him at the gallery before the doors opened. Before leaving, I douche, not because

I know we'll have sex later tonight but just in case the opportunity arises. Doing so makes me horny, so I finger myself quickly in front of the bathroom mirror. After I ejaculate I feel calmer, less burdened by existential ailments.

When I approach the gallery, I hear the buzz of conversation behind the doors. Will has to let me in, and I can feel people looking at me and then just as quickly looking away. I'm wearing a jean jacket with a pin that says "LAND BACK" on it and a patch that says "GAY 4 PAY JK ABOLISH WORK."

I scan the room for the four other BFA students featured tonight. Jules is a fabric artist who builds yarn sculptures of women stepping on men. She's in the corner with Simon, a performance artist who I hear may or may not strip naked later. Something about the tyranny of subjectivity, which is exactly what a straight undergrad would make art about. Roger, another queer, has hung up a neon sign that says LIVED EXPERIENCE—it's quite clever. Sue, the coolest person in the room, stands at the bar with a seltzer in their hand, eyeing the portraits they've installed on a movable wall. The portraits depict them as a child, appearing ungendered.

Will leads me by the hand to his paintings, a series called REZ KIDS that portrays various absurdist scenes from his reserve. One shows a cop car melting into the ground while kids run around it, laughing. Another depicts dozens of kids walking out of a lake rather than into it. I recognize the lake from my time up there, but shoes are strewn about the rocky shore in Will's painting. The facial expressions are grievous, as though some horror has just unfolded. I had no idea he was working on these paintings, each so haunting and elegantly crafted that I'm truly in awe.

"Will, my god, these are stunning," I say.

"You sure? I literally only finished them this afternoon. I can't be objective at this point."

"Trust me, the depth of thought and emotion is so present. People will love them."

As I'm speaking, a stream of people enters the gallery, and Will is shepherded away by one of his professors. He winks and says something, but the crowd is already boisterous enough to drown him out. I recognize the faces of several acquaintances, former classmates, but no one I'm close enough with to want to drum up conversation.

People drink beer and look at the art. I look at people looking at the art. Everyone is very serious about it. Will comes in and out of my field of vision. The spectacle of his importance here opens up a new kind of distance between us. For a moment I feel thinly mournful, as though I have less of a claim over him.

Someone I don't know asks if I'm related to Will and I sigh. As far as I can tell, we're the only natives in the room. It makes me feel like an object of curiosity, an art piece in my own right.

The attendees are then called to order. A man's voice booms forth from behind me, in the center of the gallery. The man looks familiar, but I can't place him.

"Welcome, everyone!" he says. "It's our pleasure to host the university's graduating class's annual thesis exhibition. This year it's called Asymmetries, an examination of how we're sometimes at odds with the world. I'd like to begin by acknowledging we're on the traditional territories of many Indigenous nations who have stewarded the land for centuries, and we thank them."

I glance over at Will and roll my eyes. He smirks.

"My name's Grant, and I'm the executive director here," he continues.

Recognition floods me. The hair, the glasses, but most obviously the name. My knees almost give out, as though I'd just been delivered terrible news. In a way, I have. Will looks at me and raises an eyebrow. I smile, shake my head to indicate there's nothing to worry about. I repeat this in my head, *nothing, nothing, nothing.*

"Tonight, we're showing the works of five emerging artists. Sue, Simon, Roger, Jules, Will, please join me for a moment, will you?"

The group surrounds him. Grant puts an arm around Will's shoulders, which Will wears ambivalently. Each student-artist shares what they hope people will take from their work, most of which I can't grasp. Then Grant permits the attendees to chatter once more, and Will and the others disperse to their de facto stations. They are nervous, but mostly they are proud.

I need to collect myself, to catch my breath, to get some air, but I don't want Will to see me step outside. I can recover and pretend nothing's wrong. I just need a second. The evening can still be spared. Will doesn't have to know anything. Maybe we'll laugh about it one day.

I walk toward the back entrance, which is where I find Grant's office. The door is open, and I peer in out of self-degrading curiosity. It's tidy, with beautiful paintings on the walls. To Grant I was something akin to a beautiful painting. So often beauty precedes an act of subjugation. When Grant reached for me in his car, he ruined me a little. The thought solidifies inside me like a weather system.

I step outside. When the door closes behind me I realize I don't want to go back in. The cold air smacks me and my chest tightens. It's all too much. I don't know what to do or where to go, so I stand in the semi-dark, eyes closed. Everything I am is cold.

I'M IN BED with my laptop on my chest. I should be in history class, but instead I'm working on a term paper on forgiveness. It's about how the government uses phrases like "sad chapter" to describe the colonial past, as though we could put it behind us like a page in a book. Most books I read stay with me, linger in my mind, changing the architecture of my thoughts. Colonial governance is a problem of interpretation, then, I intend to argue. The past is read so as to be annihilated. That is my thesis statement. *For whom is violence sad, and for whom is it a brutal inheritance?* I write.

I decided to miss class, the last one of the term, because I haven't talked to Will since the exhibition two days ago. Two days isn't very long, but for us, two young men for whom love is proof of how alive we are or aren't, it's forty-eight hours of questions, anxiety. After I arrived home that night, I sent Will a text saying I fell suddenly ill and didn't want to risk getting him sick as well. He wrote back immediately with concern, offers to deliver medication, fluids. I told him I'd see him soon enough, and he responded with a string of heart emojis.

I want to be a normal man with a normal desire to be devoted to another man. Sometimes all my being, my personhood, rails against this desire, its innocence. I feel like a man for whom innocence is a mythos from some other land. The sight of Grant at the gallery, his large arm around Will, disturbed me; it knocked my material reality askew. I realized my sexual experiences with men like Grant, men I contorted myself for, stemmed from an original wound—the wound of self-estrangement. I don't want to turn Will into a catastrophe by proximity. He checks in on me, brief texts of care, but I can't bring myself to respond.

Still, I think about how every time I kiss Will it feels as though I'm saying, "I'm here." Here in an abstract sense as well as a physical one, an exercise in devotion, in shared presence. Here, not over there, not elsewhere. Without Will, I feel less pinned to the world. That's one way to define loneliness. But I don't want to be the kind of person who's always finding new ways to define loneliness.

What if he's an antidote to my loneliness, which seems so all-encompassing? How do I alter my inner world to make that possibility feel more real?

The Indigenous relationships in my family and on my rez, relationships that span decades, are full of both turbulence and happiness, sometimes in equal measure. When faced with trouble, the possibility of repair is implicit. My friends and I joke that Indigenous love is the most chaotic force in the world. We have to desire one another in opposition to the way the white gaze makes us into objects of disdain. It's possible to injure oneself by inadequately loving someone else. I don't want this to be my fate. I want to be ready to love and not self-explode.

We've been dating for just under four months. No time at all, really. But I'm in my early twenties, and in every day is a chance to bring my future into clearer focus. I decide to head to campus, where I feel less unhinged. I get dressed.

The train station is a short walk from my apartment. I'm glad to be out of the cold and standing on the heated underground platform. When the southbound train arrives, all the cars are already full. I squeeze into one and grab on to a pole, trying not to think of its germy excess. The train jolts to a stop as it reaches the middle of the bridge that connects downtown, where I live, to the south side of the city, where the university is located. It stops at this specific point often, to allow for adjustments to be made by other trains. From here, I can see the ice's westward sprawl spanning miles. I think about an elder who told me that the river is still the most efficient way to traverse the city, even after all the geographical violence of colonialism. To traverse the water would connect me to my ancestors, but instead I'm on a train, suspended above it, suspended in a kind of disembodied space with people who won't look at each other.

It occurs to me that one also has to love despite the geographical violence of colonialism. I want to love in a way that has geographical consequences. Can love undermine a settler state? It's likely that my happiness depends on it.

AT THE UNIVERSITY, I wander through various pedways until I decide to study in the English department. As soon as I enter the building, I see Will seated at a cubicle, reading. I step back, but then stop. He looks so damn handsome, and he's wearing my hoodie. The scene reminds me that I can feel human emotion and not succumb to it.

"Tom!" He calls out when he finally notices me. He runs over. We embrace.

"Are you feeling better? I missed you in History earlier," he says, pulling back to look at me in my totality. My throat feels narrow.

"Hey, hey, what's up?" Will adds.

"Can we talk outside?" I ask.

"Totally, let me grab my things."

We huddle near a group of smokers, our breath visible, dancing on our shoulders like tiny ghosts. I decide I don't have to divulge the whole truth of my minor breakdown, which had very little to do with him. I can spare him and in so doing spare myself.

"I've been a mess the last couple days. I'm doing better now. I'm happy to see you."

I kiss him, and one of the smokers coughs. We laugh.

"I'm sorry I left the show so soon. Your work was transcendent."

"Thank you." At first his look is judicious, then it softens. "You don't have to explain anything."

His sympathy feels unearned, so I have to turn away from it. I look off toward a cluster of old houses.

"Want to go back to your place?"

I nod.

We walk quickly in the cold, but the sun is still bright, and it envelops us. It feels like a second chance. We walk along the bridge with the suicide barriers. Shortly after they were built, an artist installed sculptures of people traversing them. The work, its depiction of human determination and the failure of social policy, haunted me. I saw them still—those bodies, their ghostly shape—even though they had been taken down weeks ago.

IT'S AFTER MIDNIGHT. Will snores softly. Two used condoms lie a few feet away, and I get up to throw them in the trash. It feels surprisingly sentimental. When I return I examine Will's body, its idiom of beauty, which is perhaps now our shared idiom, something specific to us. I let the act of observation nourish me.

He stirs, opens his eyes.

"Are you watching me?"

"Possibly."

He reaches for his phone, turns it on.

"Oh fuck," he says.

"What?"

"Whoa."

"Will!"

He continues looking at his phone. I notice his body tense up. His mouth hangs open, but I can't tell if he's actually breathing. I inventory all the types of tragedy that could befall him, and I feel ethically compromised for doing so. He scrolls through a document, zooming in and out. I wait for him to say something. I reach for a pair of underwear and slowly drag them up my legs as noiselessly as possible.

"I . . . I got into an MFA program."

"That's amazing!" I say, relieved it wasn't something worse.

"It's in Vancouver."

"Oh." I feel my body and mind settling into a familiar frenzied state again. It suddenly feels nonsensical to be almost-naked. I look down at my body and shudder. "Are you going to go?"

"I, uh, I'm not sure."

Silence. I sit on the edge of the mattress, facing the wall, deciding whether to cry.

"If I went, would you come with me?" A pause. "Wait, you don't have to answer right now. Think about it. I want you to come with me. You don't have any other plans," he adds playfully.

I ground myself in the room again, feel the current between our bodies, acknowledge its potency.

"Come here," he says.

I nestle into him, under the blanket. The apartment is dark save for the glimmer of a few streetlights.

"Let's fall asleep like this, OK?" He squeezes me, pulls me closer.

"OK," I say, even though we'll be sore in the morning.

As he begins snoring again, I realize I know with total certainty that I love him. How? I will change my life for him, I will go wherever he goes.

Poetry Class

POETRY CLASS WAS HELD on Fridays on the second floor of the geography building. I liked the idea of teaching poetry there, believing as I did that poetry was its own geographic force, an act of imaginative and spatial construction. A poem could destabilize the appearance of the world's immutability. A poem, spun with enough care and power, could architect a small refuge. This has everything to do with the study of geography, the study of our built and natural environments.

Administration assigned me a dusty seminar room with outdated technology. There were still chalkboards on the walls, and in the corner was an overhead projector as old as me. I liked these anachronisms, both symptoms of the under-funding of the humanities and social sciences that in their neglect transformed into portals out of the present. It's not that I was nostalgic for the past—far from it; I wanted instead to impress upon my students a general ambivalence toward linear time. The past, the present—these were contestable categories. We experienced them simultaneously. We weren't entirely overdetermined by them, though. To be a poet one had to believe in the coexistence of these kinds of contradictory truths.

. . .

"WHAT CONSTITUTES THE POETIC IMAGINATION?" I began once the students quieted down. It was our third class; the question was far overdue. "A desire for freedom, a critique of the tyranny of materiality. Also, a love of images, a longing for an image to hold us, maybe in the way that iconic images like God or the afterlife inspire the lives of so many. Is poetry spiritual, then? What do we think?"

My students, all ten of them, stared at me, some blankly, others quizzically. I'd already begun to appreciate their attentiveness immensely, even when it was undergirded by confusion. After a decade or so of teaching, the company of students had become an integral part of my social life. Our conversations about art and literature had shaped who I was as much as my partner or my upbringing had. My students taught me to undermine institutional authority, to be vulnerable even when I felt guarded. I've tried to act as generously and rigorously as possible. I've tried to persuade them to see writing as one method by which to testify to their right to exist in the world.

"Are you asking if poetry has something to do with the soul?" asked one student.

"I suppose so, though the soul can mean something nonreligious."

"I don't think there's a fixed relation between the two," the student continued. "If that were the case, wouldn't poetry always be about ethics?"

"Determining what's worthy of reverence or poetic observation is an ethical judgment," I said. "A poetic life is a beautiful life, and beauty is ultimately about freedom, right? Throughout the twentieth century, Canadian poets were writing pastoral poems that celebrated country life and the glory of nature. The ability to aestheticize the pasture is presupposed by dispossession, by colonization. One could argue, then, that Indigenous life fell out of these poets' frames of ethical consideration. In fact, Indigenous suffering had to continue unabated in order for their work to cohere. That's a vision of poetry that is unbeautiful, in my opinion. Maybe poetry that requires dispossession isn't poetry after all but propaganda. I want to insist on a notion of poetry and of art-making more broadly that is against violence and for shared flourishing. I think that implicates the human spirit, our ethical positions."

The class remained silent, but there was an air of contemplation. I knew I wouldn't win everyone over. Many had enrolled in the program to professionalize their writing, to have time to write a book with an eye toward publication. Past students grew tired of my abstract bent, or so I read in my evaluations at the end of every term. I was interested in an education in desire, all the same. Alongside writing poems and loving and being loved, it was my life's duty.

≡

THAT EVENING, I READ on the couch while my partner, S, worked on his laptop beside me—a domestic scene I was affixed to with total security. To be a domestic subject situated in a common trope didn't have to be distressing. In fact, I felt narratively sound in my life, a rarity as of late. The new teaching term had energized me, jolted me out of a stupor. To teach poetry reminded me of the pleasure of knowledge and therefore of the pleasure of being in the world with others. S got up to go to the bathroom, and not long thereafter his phone vibrated on the coffee table, face up. The sender didn't have a name, just numbers. "thanks for meeting the other evening, it was a lovely time." I felt light-headed. Was this evidence of an affair? Or just a friendly message from an acquaintance? That I couldn't decide felt like a bad omen. When S's footsteps approached, I collected myself and turned my attention back to the book. He picked up his phone, but nothing specific registered on his face. Still, all the language in me crumpled. Language was no longer something that put me in communion with others; it was a distant idea. He put the phone in his pocket and scanned the local newspaper beside me, something he'd done on innumerable evenings. My thoughts became wild and intrusive. Maybe innumerability was the problem. Maybe our shared life had grown vague and monotonous and I hadn't noticed. I thought that was the whole point. After twelve years of coupledom, we were supposed to be boring and ordinary. We were supposed to face the second half of our lives with a determined modesty. We were supposed to derive pleasure from the quiet repetition of our days. I hoped that beauty could arise out of that quiet repetition; this was the sort of thing I'd say to my students. Perhaps, though, it was in the nature of a man to desire errantly. I channeled my libidinal energy into S as well as into the work of poetry—to map the utopian was, in a sense, an erotic act, another form of social reproduction. What outlets of release did S make use of?

S had worked in marketing at a small publishing house since before we met. The authors he worked with changed every year, but the terms of that work never did: he had to help sell books. More often than not he struggled to do even that. He couldn't figure out why people bought or didn't buy books anymore.

My own books, three poetry collections, sold poorly in a Canadian market that generally neglected poetry. We'd talked about the Canadian market endlessly over the years. Making beautiful books wasn't enough, S concluded. He had to convince newspapers and magazines and TV producers that the books his company published were experiences unto themselves. One should be changed inalterably having read them, he would tell possible clients and stakeholders. Whenever he said this, I often wondered, do people really want to be changed inalterably? A book of poetry was different from the activity of poetry; the former was a symptom of the latter, they weren't analogous. That poetry had a revolutionary demand—one of Audre Lorde's enduring lessons—meant that the categories of salability and marketability were ultimately antithetical and irrelevant. S had to see books as profit- or debt-producing objects. To him, it was a normal way to view the world. It was one of the fundamental differences that we again and again had to confront. He would say I was overly seduced by theoretical paradigms. *That's the whole point*, I would say, *I'm trying to embody them*.

. . .

IN BED S FELL ASLEEP almost as soon as he shut his eyes, and I sat up awake next to him. His breathing body confounded me. In no way did it register the trauma of a punctured fantasy, the one I was living out. I was less a man and more the wound left by the trauma of a punctured fantasy. I could hear the chatter of passersby through the window that faced the residential street. I felt like a passerby in my own life. The present was a brief glimpse, an indiscernible conversation. I would have to discuss my life in the third person so as not to suggest epistemic authority.

I thought about all the books we had amassed and blended into one library; it would be painstaking to dismantle them. I regarded our library with a sense of wonder, how tangibly it represented our interconnectedness. If I wanted to quantify our love, I could do so in pages. I thought about staying with him until I died simply to not have to pull apart the bookshelves.

Eventually I gave up on sleep, rolled out of bed, and crept into the kitchen. S's phone was charging on the counter; he liked to be at a distance from it during the night. I contemplated sifting through his photos and texts. I knew his passcode just as he knew mine. I looked through the sliding door in the living area instead and saw that the sky was clear. One of the tragedies of my life was that I couldn't see the moon from any window in our apartment at any time of the year. A poet must look at the moon sometimes to remember that there is a trace of the cosmic already inside him. I went out onto the patio and leaned over the small fence to see it, but it was mostly eclipsed by an apartment tower. I scanned the area, dominated by housing complexes that were constructed prior to and in the wake of the Olympics at the start of the decade. I could see a bit of the inlet, which was so contaminated by human waste that the seawall often smelled of sewage. One day the neighborhood would end up entirely underwater. I would be long gone when that happened. So much was built to be destroyed, I thought, thinking of Elizabeth Bishop's famous line, "so many things seem filled with the intent to be lost." There is so little we could do in the face of that kind of death drive.

Back in the house, I saw the long arc of the relationship from a new perspective. There was a beginning and a middle and an end. It was a simple story.

The beginning: S and I met the weekend I moved to the west coast from Alberta. I was using the wireless internet at a café when he sat down beside me and asked about the book beside my laptop. It was an experimental novel that had won a big award the year before. He told me he'd found it boring and disembodied. I told him that I generally read a book on its own terms, so it was rare that I disavowed one or found it "bad." I was nervous and caught unawares, so I rambled about postmodernism and the spoils of plot and the political uses of illegibility. I appreciated his honesty, and he found my loquaciousness endearing. He invited me to a reading he'd heard about from an artist friend. Coincidentally, the reading was being put on by my department and I was the featured reader. He sat in the front row, wide-eyed, as I read poems about cruising and intergenerational trauma and loneliness. I couldn't help but look at him the whole time. After the reading, I went back to his place. We had sex, easy and effortlessly, and after we finished we lay awake for hours talking and laughing and then fucking some more.

The middle consisted of long drives and literary parties and family visits and even more sex. There was joy and splendor and anger and bitterness but mostly there was calm. He sold books, I published books. He read my poems and was jealous when I wrote about old lovers and shy and avoidant when I wrote about him. We gained weight and he went bald and I kept wearing skinny jeans despite the trend expiring. He took up crosswords and I learned how to play tennis, albeit not very well. I found new things to admire about him, how he made a tradition of taking out my books from various libraries because there was a potential small financial benefit, how he taught himself French so we could vacation in Paris and not feel like interlopers, how he always kept his eyes open when we kissed (this seemed most important to me now). We counted our blessings and kept some plants alive, and we had our exquisite moments when all the good in the world was alive in our bodies.

That a whole decade could be reduced to a paragraph was awful and ordinary and ordinarily awful.

At last, I became drowsy. I tiptoed back into our bedroom where S was uncovered and splayed out on top of the sheets. He was naked, and his round and hairy butt was the first thing I saw once my eyes adjusted to the dark. Oh, how I adored his butt. Despite the text, despite the uncertainty of the coming days, I was glad to see him there. I wanted to lie beside him, to pull the blanket over him. I still loved him in the present tense.

≡

THAT WEEK I ASKED MY STUDENTS to write a poem in the language of rain on pieces of paper I had cut up into small squares. Rain on the west coast was as much a part of the fabric of existence as economic precarity. There were months recently during which it rained every day. Rain made us weepy, but it also made us introspective. It made us decide if we loved ourselves or not. Rain left an aroma of desire in the air. It was desire incarnate, something that could leave us drenched and shivering. Desire could fall on us without reprieve.

My students wanted more direction. "What do you mean by the language of rain?"

I tugged at the collar of my button-up, looked out the window. It had rained all morning. The patter echoed throughout the geography building. "The language of rain is a language of ephemerality. It isn't about permanency or plumbing the depths of the self. Rain is communal: we all experience it similarly. Rain transmits information. Is it possible to capture that information in a poem? Might a poem be the only way to do so? What does the rain tell us? What is its tone, its mood?"

My students seemed satisfied with these remarks, though they were entirely improvised. "Think of our lesson on Yoko Ono's writing, think of her little instructional poems. She writes for and as natural elements. She displaces the human as the locus of poetic agency. Think of the rain as your intended audience. Think of the rain as the texture of your thinking and speaking."

As they scribbled and erased and rewrote, I looked at the contents of my bag, which I had purchased at an Indigenous boutique on a visit to the prairies for a literary festival. I had been invited to read from my second book on a panel with poets who had also recently published second books. The host asked questions about writer's block and self-doubt and redundancy. The conversation mostly centered on uncertainty, something I've never imbued with poetic value. I was asked the last question, likely because I hadn't said much. "What can Canadians do to be better allies to Indigenous peoples?" It was a question I'd had to field at several festivals, though it was seldom on topic. It elicited a physiological response, made me uneasy. I was tired. My first thought was that we had to dismantle the category of the Canadian. To be Canadian required a degree of violence—the violence of maintaining the nation as a dispossessive force. But all I could say was "I don't know. I don't know." The question was an anthropological one, not a poetic one. I refused those terms of engagement. The exercise I presented to my students seemed also to be about disrupting the anthropological gaze. It was about resisting objectification and romanticization; it was about being the rain.

After thirty minutes, I asked my students to pack up and meet me outside the building with their poems in hand. Once outside, I directed them to place the poems on the ground so that the rain could dissolve them. No one protested. We stood silently in a semicircle as the poems slowly broke down and their words no longer looked like words. We stood there elegiacally for the rest of class, saying nothing. By surrendering to the rain, the poems eventually became an indiscriminate part of the earth. I too wanted to become an indiscriminate part of the earth. It was a fundamentally mournful undertaking.

≡

A FEW DAYS AFTER I discovered the text message, S and I got into an argument on the drive home from dinner with friends. He tensed up when I made a comment about how the structure of whiteness shaped some of my students' writing. He wanted me to be more empathetic, to consider the fact of peoples' bodies and their good intentions. He thought I judged my students too harshly. Again, theory came up as an object of derision. He was more riled up than normal; I was caught by surprise. I had tried to communicate to him in the past that I needed space to air my frustrations about racism without him feeling personally affronted. To be in a relationship with a non-Indigenous person took work. Because I loved him, I was happy to do the work. I believed that love between an Indigenous man and a white man wasn't doomed to be marginalizing. That night, however, I told him I didn't have it in me to argue about whiteness. That wounded him. "I'm not arguing about whiteness," he said quietly. I rested my head against the passenger seat window and sighed. Moisture dispersed across my face at once.

S didn't look at me again until morning.

≡

I CANCELED CLASS the week after the rain exercise. In an email, I informed my students that I was feeling under the weather. In truth, I felt myself giving up on language. I was becoming moved less and less to speak. I was becoming a poet with nothing at all to say. Sentences were boulders I didn't want to carry. I wanted to throw my sentences into the ocean and watch them sink.

≡

I WAITED FOR S TO ARRIVE HOME. When I taught, I was on campus until the evening, so our Fridays were open-ended. S and I seldom spent them together. Still, I worried over his absence. There had been no text message or phone call. I didn't want to contact him, I didn't want to oppress him with my misery, which I still hadn't given words to. Unexpressed misery was my private knowledge. I knew that I could end up guarding it to the point of self-subjugation. It would be akin to the experience of being trapped in a novel, entranced by my own interiority. I'd never imagined my life as novelistic because I tried to live in the future tense, as most poets do.

I was seated at the kitchen table, which was small enough to fit into the narrow space between the kitchen and the living room. Domestic life on the west coast was a matter of shrinking oneself and one's belongings; it was a counter to sentimentality. From where I was stationed, I could see the handful of photographs of us that we'd kept over the years, each a defense of the sentimental. They captured our falling in love. S was the first to say he loved me. He said it after sex during a short vacation on a nearby island. In a photo taken on that trip, we're in a small cabin washed out by the sun; we look like horny ghosts.

"Hey, I love you," he'd said, looking at the ceiling.

I waited a couple minutes. The room closed in around me. I put my hand on his hairy chest. One of his nipples was erect. There was still semen on his belly, the smell of it permeating the air. He was shorter and thinner than I was. There was a fragility in the way he inhabited space that made me want to be gentle and soft-hearted.

"I love you more," I said, as a child might.

That bit carried on until the recent past. Perhaps it was no longer cute. One of us might love the other less. We didn't need to do the math.

I was reading on the couch when S finally walked in. It had been dark for hours already.

"Where were you?" I asked without peeling my eyes from the page.

"Oh, out with colleagues," he said. "Celebrating a new publication."

He walked over and kissed my forehead. "I'm jumping in the shower," he said as he disappeared down the hallway. By the time I went to bed he was asleep. I had an impulse to wake him up, to ask him to help carry my anguish. A relationship was as much about carrying someone else's pain as it was about sharing in their joy. It seemed to me I had been deserted to tend to my own woundedness, self-exiled in the apartment most days while he was out with friends and colleagues. I realized, though, that he wasn't the sole cause of my sadness; it preceded the possibility of an affair. It took the possibility of an affair for me to see the ugly landscape of my suffering. My personhood had soured, and with it my creativity, my language. Hours later, I managed to fall asleep too.

I WANTED TO CANCEL the subsequent class, but news would've spread in the department and the thought of disappointing my students was overwhelming. In class, I wrote a prompt on the chalkboard: *We build little worlds wherever we go, often with the desire to not be destroyed by life.* "A poem," I told them, "is at the very least a record of one's survival. It brings about an *I*. It is a process of generation and survival."

One student said something that struck me, left me speechless: "A beautiful sentence is a reason to live. We write because we want to keep living."

It occurred to me that it had been months since I'd last written a poem.

≡

S HAD BEEN MYSTERIOUSLY AWAY AGAIN. He looked handsome when he at last returned home. He'd lost weight over the last month, having returned to the gym after a period of inactivity. I wanted to kiss him and maybe even go down on him; it was the first erotic urge I'd had since before the start of the term. I slid a hand up his shirt. He put down his phone and touched my face. It was both affectionate and pitiful. We kissed.

"Not so heavy," he said, pushing me back. "It's nothing," he said in response to my pained expression. "I'm tired is all. Maybe tomorrow?"

"How long has it been?" I asked.

"Since what?"

"Since we did anything remotely sexual together?" I knew I was being petulant, but I couldn't stop myself.

S sighed and sat down at the kitchen table.

"What?" I shot back.

"I thought we'd have more time," he said.

"What do you mean?"

"Before we got to this point." He gestured at the living room. To me it seemed as it always had. "I've always thought that to love someone you had to find a way to see them up close and from afar and admire both views. But I feel like these days I'm stuck in that bird's-eye view. I'm in your periphery." The statement filled the house like vapor.

"I'm not sure I follow the metaphor," I said. "You're saying that you live at a distance from me?"

"Exactly."

"Why haven't you said anything before? Why hold that in?"

"What was I supposed to do? You can't just reel someone back in, make them more present. I certainly don't have or want that power."

"Fuck." I sat down, my eyes wet with tears. The truth of what was happening was more devastating than infidelity. We no longer inhabited a united world of feeling. If he'd slept with another man, it was likely a way of convincing himself of what he already knew: that our collective *I* had disintegrated.

"You're somewhere else," S said. "You're not here with me in the room most of the time. We've splintered off; it honestly feels like we've already moved on from each other."

He was right. Nothing could dispute that fact. Still, I'd been content to orbit him, even if indifferently, and I could've for a long time. Alas, not everyone was up to that task. I couldn't blame him for wanting out, something different, more exhilarating.

I looked over at the sliding door and saw a trace of moonlight reflected off a nearby condominium. I stared at it for several minutes.

≣

I RETURNED TO CLASS, not with added agony but roused once again by the knowledge that language was all I had. If I gave up on it, I'd be nothing.

≣

S AND I GRADUALLY SEPARATED. He stayed with a friend or in the guest room as we figured out how to be individuals again. He planned to relocate to a less expensive part of the city, into a rental he could afford on his own salary. I saw him once or twice a week, in passing. We continued not to talk about our problems, perhaps finally giving in to their unfixability, our lack of willingness to remake ourselves. It seemed to me that most relationships ended because someone didn't want to become someone else.

I returned home after the last class of the term to discover that S had retrieved most of his belongings and left for good. I surveyed the bedroom and the bathroom and felt a sense of ease at the whittling down of objects, furniture, and clothing. I would have more space; another man could implant his things. I checked the study last. He'd left most of his books. The library remained essentially as it was. I didn't know if he would come back for them, as there was no note. I touched the spines of some of his books, then some of mine. We owned classics and works in translation and contemporary North American writing. An entire bookcase was dedicated to poetry. I felt connected to an immense human tradition, and I knew that I wasn't truly alone.

Sex Lives: An Anonymous Chorus

The first time I had sex with a man was at a truck stop two hours southeast of the reserve and one hour from Edmonton. It was 1980, and I was barely an adult. The whole time the man held me like a fist, pushing my face against a wall tiled with yellow flowers. I tried to count the yellow flowers but they were too blurry. Someone knocked on the locked door, asking to use the washroom. The man covered my mouth with his hand, which tasted like dirt and coffee and whatever lubricant he'd brought with him. It was the lubricant that tasted the foulest. He spoke to the person on the other side of the door in a formal tone, out of sync with what was happening in the bathroom—he continued to thrust aggressively into me. I had to suppress groans of pleasure and displeasure. I thought of my short life as one long groan of pleasure and displeasure.

When the man came, he wiped his dick then flushed the toilet paper. After that, he washed his face with cold water. I noticed he was wearing cowboy boots. They reminded me of my father's. I looked at him through the mirror, which made his face seem newer. A calmness settled across it. I wanted to kiss him. I wondered if what we had just done constituted intimacy. If not, what was it?

He didn't look back at me, still on the floor. We fucked because of deliberate glances, the right timing. Was that enough to be something meaningful? Before I could say anything, my legs still trembling, he walked out of the bathroom.

My body ached the rest of the drive home.

My longing had at last been externalized. Something opaque about me had clarified. I was no longer doomed to unknowing. Alas, knowing itself was a kind of violence. I decided that if I were to desire and be desired, it would come at some cost, there would be some act of forfeiture.

For a while, whenever I made the drive between the reserve and the city, I stopped at the truck stop to see if that man was there. He never was. Eventually I realized that my waiting had less to do with him and more to do with me. I desired his cruelty. I wanted my face to collide with a blur of yellow. I wanted to be less beholden to my life, to be less of a person. This escapist drive came naturally to me. The fantasy allowed me to feel less estranged from the world than I actually was.

2.

I fell in love with a boy in high school. It was the early nineties in northern Alberta, so we met in secret. The secrecy of our relationship made it volatile and all-consuming. After graduation, he went off to college and I stayed at home to help my mom raise my younger siblings on the reserve. I thought about him endlessly, my thoughts constituting a whole inner world. He drove up from the city every other weekend to see me. We would find a secluded stretch of beach on the lake and make out. In the winter, I snuck him into my bedroom through the window. I had shoveled snow against the exterior to make it possible; no one asked about the footprints. All those years, no one knew what we were and we didn't have the power to name it ourselves. I never asked about his college life. It hurt less to be ignorant. When I had saved enough money to buy a car, I drove to the city to spend time with him. We slept on the twin mattress in his dorm room. We slept terribly but that was proof of our commitment to each other. I left during the early mornings so his friends wouldn't find out. These few days a week felt enormous to me. We made a life that way for the duration of his degree. We lost touch after he moved to another province to teach. When he told me about the opportunity, I didn't stop him. It paid too much. We were both so poor. I couldn't ask him to move back north, to return to the deprivation of his childhood. He deserved better. I believed that more than I believed anything else.

I found out he died not long after moving. He had been sick for a handful of years. The news pummeled me. It confirmed something about the world I wasn't able to fully let sink in until then. I spent most of my twenties and thirties in mourning. It was all I knew how to do.

3.

I was dozing off, but the buzzing of a dating app kept me awake. A man in the west end invited me to his place. He asked if it was OK if his friend joined. I was intrigued; I'd never had a threesome before. I said no in the end—the friend didn't want to send a selfie and I had a rule against anonymous sex. The man said that was OK, he would ask him to leave. I drove for forty minutes on mostly empty streets. It was Thursday night. It was late summer. I was horny; I was nervous. I kept scanning the photos he sent me. Some were pixelated, so I assumed they were old. I didn't care because he was attractive. I wanted to have sex with an attractive man. I thought it would make me less miserable.

He lived in an apartment building near a reserve, which I could see in the distance. The city and the reserve weren't always so close; suburban sprawl brought the former to the edge of the latter. Had the reserve not already been established there, the city might've continued sprawling westward. The reserve's proximity became another hang-up in the city's colonial imagination. I, on the other hand, relished its defiant permanency.

When I arrived at the complex, I opened the app and saw that there were several men in the vicinity. One had already messaged me, sent photos. I was still looking at the grid of users when the man knocked on my car window. It startled me. He waved, said he recognized me from my profile picture. He was indeed older than he let on, but he was handsome all the same. My dick was already getting hard.

I got out and walked with him up a few flights of stairs. He kept grabbing at my ass. He led me to the end of a long hallway. His unit was the last on the right. The building was quiet, and a stale smell emanated from the carpet. The door was slightly ajar. When we stepped inside there was another man sitting on a couch. I froze. The man told me that this was his friend, Anthony. He said he preferred threesomes, so he didn't ask Anthony to leave. He said Anthony really wanted to fuck me, that I should feel lucky. I looked over at Anthony when he said this, but he didn't react. Like me, Anthony was native. He was wearing a baseball cap and baggy clothing. He reminded me of the men up north, my cousins. We resembled each other.

The man closed the door behind me and began to undress. He said he was going to take a shower because it had been a long day. He asked if I wanted to join him and I said no. Anthony also declined. Anthony looked afraid; his hands shook. I scanned the apartment. It was essentially empty save for the couch and whatever was in the bedroom. The kitchen looked unused. Beer cans were piled in a corner. I could smell the man's cologne. The apartment was lit by a single lamp and the glow of the bathroom ceiling light.

I waited to know what to do. I thought an ancient survival instinct might eventually kick in. My head pounded. I noticed Anthony was fiddling with his hands. His facial expression was vacant. We looked as though we'd just suffered an unspeakable trauma together. I peered into the hallway to glimpse the man in the shower. He was cleaning his ass.

I told Anthony I'd left lube in the car and had to go fetch it. Anthony said they had lube. I said I left my phone and wanted to have it on me. I was already out the door before he could respond. I decided I didn't want to die. It was the first time the desire was so solid inside me. All it took was an experience of sexual degradation.

As I opened the door to my car I heard someone shut the apartment's main entrance. I turned around and saw Anthony. I wanted to speed off, but I felt a minor allegiance to him, suspected the other man was the mastermind. I got into the car and rolled down the window. Anthony asked if I could give him a ride home, he didn't want to stay over at the man's place. He lived on the reserve. Buses didn't run this late. He looked shaken, so I said yes. On the road, I tried to make small talk but all he uttered were directions: left, right, past this intersection. I asked how he knew the man. He told me his name was Doug, and that he was a little fucked up. I asked what he meant.

He said Doug seemed to always find young native guys on the apps. He often got aggressive with them. Anthony lifted his shirt and showed me a bruise on his left side. He said it was from Doug's foot when he was fucking him the other night. He didn't listen when Anthony told him to ease up, then to stop. I asked him why he was there just now. Anthony said he wasn't sure; he didn't have anything else to do tonight. No one on the apps seemed interested, he said. I understood the subtext: no one wants to fuck a native guy who looks native as fuck. This wasn't quite the truth but it felt real all the same. We had both wanted to fill some existential void—and failed.

I pulled into a townhouse complex. Anthony directed me to a unit with a blue van in the driveway. A TV glowed in the large window. He said he lived with his mom, so he couldn't host anyone. He waited. He leaned in to kiss me; I let him. His mouth tasted like cigarettes. He thanked me for the ride and, as he got out of the car, asked if we could hang out sometime. I told him I didn't know what I was doing anymore. He stared at me and frowned. After a pause, he shut the passenger door.

4.

In England, my life was split between my studies and sex. I had an intellectual life and a sex life—sometimes they intertwined. In the heart of empire, I was lonely. I thought by moving to England I would find a new happiness. But people here were racist too. No one knew that I was native, so I was the target of an array of prejudices. I joked that I was a ghost haunting the streets of Oxford. The violence of colonization continued even in my spectral form.

One man at a café told me to go back to where I came from because I sat at a table he had been eyeing. Gladly, I thought. I wondered if, in a roundabout philosophical way, I was inextricably enmeshed with the UK. I was a product of British invasion, after all. I was a post-contact native. Maybe I had agreed to study at Oxford so as to return to the primal wound of my making.

I had a bad habit of thinking in a roundabout philosophical way, but I was still attuned to my material conditions of living. Some of my peers, who came from other colonies (current and former), seemed incapable of doing this. One time, I got in a heated argument with a wealthy American who wanted to convince me that history progressed by way of luck or chance and according to random bouts of change that we couldn't anticipate. I countered that political advances were made by marginalized people who organized according to their desires for freedom. He dismissed me and continued his conversation with someone else. The next day he messaged me on Facebook to say that he felt that I was being too emotional to have a sound debate with but that he still found me attractive and would like to hook up sometime. I blocked him.

≡

IN THE THROES OF MY BRITISH INVISIBILITY, Grindr made me feel visible in an erotic way. I used it all day, even in class, even at dinner with friends.

My first fuck buddy was an anthropology graduate student from Estonia who wanted to write as sparsely as possible. He believed that sparse writing was pure, clean. The first night we met he asked if he could sleep over. My bed was so small I managed to sleep only in short bursts. His snoring enraged me, but I did nothing with my rage. In the morning he gave me his number and kissed me on the lips. After he left, I walked into a pasture and felt rabid. I texted him and asked if he would like to go on a proper date. He replied that night to say that he was interested only in sex. I replied immediately to say that I understood and would love to have sex again. The next day, he rode his bike over after class and I licked his armpits in the shower. In my bed, he said he could only come if he choked me. I said no—he didn't come, neither did I. He wanted to stay over again, but I had class in the morning. We talked for hours before he left. He told me he had studied the linguistic properties of some tribes in South America. I told him white men loved to turn me into a story without an ending. I was someone who just—

MY SECOND FUCK BUDDY was an Irish man who was cheating on his wife. He fucked me as though I were an object. He fucked me so hard I felt certain the collision of flesh reverberated throughout the dormitory. I avoided my floormates for days after. One time, he forgot to take off his wedding ring. It was obvious he used sex with me to forget himself. In this way, we had synchronous desires.

MY FINAL FUCK BUDDY was an older man who lived on a houseboat. The first thing he said to me was that he loved my body. I liked how considerate he was: he always took the used condoms with him when he left. I never asked why. Once, we went to a bathhouse together on a Tuesday afternoon. There was only one other man there whom we made out with until I grew bored. I meant to go over to his place, even to just feel the water beneath me, but it never happened. We worked because we were both disconnected—me from my homeland, him from the present. To touch each other was to draw a line of continuity into the future—a last-ditch attempt. Years later, I thought about writing an essay or a poem about him but when I sat down to write all I had were a few sentences. Sometimes all we have of someone are a few glistening sentences.

ſ.

The professor visited my dorm room during his lunch hour every day this week. He arrived at 12:05 and left by 12:55. Each time, we did something different, but the act always increased in intensity in relation to the previous day. Yesterday, he wanted me to record us fucking, so I did. I sent him the video over WhatsApp—none of our identifying features were visible (that was my caveat). Today, he wanted to urinate on me. We were in the shower stall in the shared bathroom. He hung up his blazer and suit pants and I left my clothes crumpled in the corner. They were already getting wet.

He was in the Department of Criminology—he didn't tell me this; I looked it up after our first meeting. According to his faculty webpage, he studied crime in rural America. He had published a scholarly monograph. The internet suggested it had gone mostly unreviewed and unread. I was in the Department of Politics. I'm sure he also looked this up. He knew I wouldn't have to take a class with him.

In the shower, the professor kissed me. His kiss was too heavy; the taste of coffee invaded my mouth. I pushed him away gently.

"I need to piss now," he said.

I looked down at his penis, which was semi-hard. I noticed he had shaved his pubes that morning, which seemed strange to me. He hadn't done so all week.

"OK," I said. "Anywhere but my mouth."

The professor aimed at my chest. His urine was a deep yellow and smelled pungent. I wanted to retch but didn't want to embarrass him. I held my breath until he finished. He became hard in the process. I jerked him off until he ejaculated. I watched the semen swirl down the drain with the water.

Did I want any of this? Why wasn't I able to figure it out?

6.

When the man pulled the condom out of his butt, I looked away. It reminded me too much of a hook being pried from a fish's mouth.

Remember: a man is a fable that doesn't necessarily convey a moral.

We must have looked ridiculous—our jeans still balled up at our feet.

Young Adults

SINCE MOVING, SEVERAL PEOPLE have asked me which city I think is better, Edmonton or Vancouver. Both are plagued by the terrors of capital (resource extraction and endless unaffordable housing developments, respectively), but Edmonton comprises part of my ancestral territory. My Cree heart will always ache for it, even when I'm there. Tom and I rent a one-bedroom in what was advertised as a building with "historic character"—historic because it hasn't yet been bulldozed in the name of gentrification, but it will be one day. I don't so much feel a part of something historic as I do feel corrupted by history's eventual demolition. When I say this to Tom, he writes it down. "History's eventual demolition," he repeats. It sounds pretentious when he says it, but I'm not embarrassed; in fact, I feel acknowledged in an intellectual manner, an acknowledging that I crave from Tom and no one else.

Tom has decided to be a writer. He enrolled in an introductory course at a local writing center that will start in the winter. He also decided not to work full-time, partly because my fellowship covers rent and my reserve's living allowance covers most of our groceries. "I have lived off less," he says about his slow stream of income from the part-time tutoring he does at the Indigenous education college down the street. Sometimes his optimism is encouraging, other times it's a ridiculous fiction. Luckily, I can hold a lot of space for that which has a slant relationship to the truth, for that which agitates and seeks to reimagine the facts of our material existence. It's a small political thrill, one of many at the core of our relationship. We arrived in Vancouver knowing we would stay for only two years. Because of this, we can sensibly make miscalculations of living and not be doomed. We can luxuriate in the spectacle of sudden change, at least for a little while.

Tom agreed to move with me to the west coast on the condition that we'd return to the prairies as soon as possible. I had no intention of staying put in Vancouver, so I agreed. We would both be uprooted from the sites of our personhood, but I had reason to believe that we could function as small anchors for each other in the interstices of our shifting selves.

≣

I ARRIVE LATE to my Theory of Art seminar and sit at the edge of a misshapen circle of tiny student desks. The instructor, a middle-aged woman named Wendy wearing a short velvet dress and faux moccasins, is gesturing excitedly as she delivers a lecture on feminist theories of visual culture. The structuring essay for the class is Laura Mulvey's famous 1975 "Visual Pleasure and Narrative Cinema," which I read last night and found myself mostly nodding along to when I wasn't bogged down by the heavy psychoanalytic language. The jargon at first felt like a thicket I had to slash my way through until I remembered the language was a stylistic choice, one I had to honor with close attention—not unlike when I look at a painting in a gallery until I feel as though I've taken on its texture and worn it like skin.

Mulvey makes the argument that under patriarchy women are "the bearer[s] of meaning, not maker[s] of meaning." Cinema, Mulvey argues, positions the "female form" as that which is to be looked at, emphasizing the drama of "sexual difference," or the "threat of castration" (outdated concepts, in my opinion, but I decide not to mention that in class).

"The male gaze structures the viewing experience and forces all to indulge in the pleasure of the subjugated woman, even other women," Wendy says.

I think about what viewing experience I want my art to elicit. Obviously, not a castration fear. I want to examine the coloniality of the present, which falls outside the purview of Mulvey's essay. She is articulating something about whiteness, not just heteropatriarchy. When I make this point in class, some of my peers nod in agreement, but Wendy asks me to say more; I detect a slight tinge of annoyance in her voice.

"The desire to control time and space through film must bear some relationship to the desire to control history and land, which are settler desires," I say.

Wendy listens thoughtfully but doesn't add anything. In both art schools I've studied at now, colonialism barely coheres as an object of serious inquiry. Neither art nor the imagination more generally exceed the colonial context. I keep saying this to people. I'm not sure how else to put it. My creative practice is a study of the ways Indigenous peoples make total conquest impossible. So, I hope the viewing experience can elicit in onlookers a desire to build a new world. But I'm uncertain whether art school can teach me how to elicit in others this desire. The moment passes before I get a chance to say this.

WHEN I RETURN to the apartment, Tom sits at the table in his underwear, hunched over a laptop. The room smells stale, overly human. The September light is warm; it illuminates Tom's disheveled and oily hair when I part a few curtains. He finishes typing and looks over at me. I have the idea that it would be hot to give him a blow job under the table, but I don't.

"Why did I opt to remain in the Art School Industrial Complex?" I bemoan.

Tom laughs. "Because we're all at the whim of our secret longings to fit in and be acknowledged."

"So true, bestie."

"Class suck today?"

"Mostly I'm just experiencing the limit of my instructor's interests. I know grad school is meant to cultivate a desire to delight in someone else's interests, but that's easier said than done."

I empty the contents of my backpack on the table, including next week's reading: a long essay about commodity fetishism and the economization of interest. I make a note to flesh out the various valences of "interest" that have appeared around me.

"What've you been working on?"

Tom hesitates. "Oh, this weird story-thing I can't seem to get a handle on."

He resumes typing as soon as he completes the sentence.

"It's nice out," I say.

"I think I should keep working—I have a tutoring session this evening, so I want to get in as much writing as I can this afternoon. Sorry, dear."

"Totally," I reply, slightly wounded. I'm still getting used to being rebuffed. It occurs to me that our relationship is now in a phase where our togetherness hums with less meaning; it's no longer an event when we're in the same room. I sit down and pick up the essay. I glaze over a few sentences, then put it down. Adulthood requires that we stick with activities and relations even when they don't feel meaningful. Banality acquires its own form of meaningfulness. I watch Tom nod rhythmically while rereading his own sentences in his head.

TOM RETURNS LATE in the evening, after I've begun readying for bed. He explains that he helped several students rewrite essays about native literary history, a topic he isn't an expert in but has a few passionate theories about nonetheless. Tom had to overperform his knowledge, but the central cause of his exhaustion was grammar. He's been agonizing over whether to zero in on grammar and syntax during his tutoring sessions, seeing that they were imposed on us as a symptom of colonization. English, after all, is a language of settlement, one we were coaxed into. Some native students rebel against it and Tom sympathizes, understanding the rebellion as a political undertaking, one he sees himself a part of as well. He knows, however, that instructors will deduct marks if there are too many errors, and thus their grades will suffer. Today he chose to put aside his politics and do the work of grammatical instruction, which took several hours.

"I'm so fucking tired," he says. "But I'm going to write a bit before bed. Don't wait up." He kisses my forehead. I try to catch his gaze, but he rushes off. The typing starts immediately. I read a bit, then turn off the bedside lamp.

· · ·

I WAKE UP before the alarm goes off. To avoid waking Tom, I roll gently off the bed to retrieve my phone. I'm not sure how long he stayed up. I watch him adjust to the space that opens up beside him and decide not to shower so as not to generate too much sound. I quietly splash warm water on my face. When I retrieve my books and supplies, I notice how youthful Tom looks when he's asleep, whirring with possibility. I feel less possible in comparison, even though I'm just a few years older.

I set out for my studio, located on the edge of campus. My first critique is next week for a workshop called The Practice of Art. I've sat through two critiques now and both times was surprised by the intensity of consideration (good and bad), something I hadn't experienced in undergrad. Here, the artist whose work is up for critique can't respond—this is called the "cone of silence rule." I needed to finish my painting as well as work on steeling myself. It isn't that I'm averse to critique, but that young artists are vicious. There's a pleasure in spotting someone else's errors. It's how one demonstrates their aesthetic superiority. In a way, critique is a theater of subordination.

I share studio space with three other students. My cubicle is sparsely furnished with a lamp, a fake plant, and an easel in the corner. The painting I'm almost finished with is more personal than my other work: a rendering of a photograph of my mother as a teenager, leaning against a faded-blue pickup truck. The photo was taken a few days before my mother met my father, when she was working several odd jobs and saving money to move to Edmonton. She ended up getting pregnant with me a couple months later, so she stayed on the reserve, not wanting to raise a child away from her family. I want to capture the joy that radiates from my mother in the photograph, a version of her I never knew.

The painting is my attempt to extend my mother's happiness.

It has always been my belief that to paint something is to imbue it with life. So, I paint the past; I paint the whole damn world.

. . . .

IN THE EVENING, Tom and I attend a reading at a small, cramped bookstore. It's late September but still warm out. Everyone is sweating. The event is in celebration of a local writer's latest novel, which has been nominated for a literary prize. The reading goes on for longer than I think it should. Too much description, too much dialogue—I feel drenched in decontextualized information. It's a little like being on the internet all day. When did novels start to feel like the internet—so heavy, and so unlike paintings?

There's applause when the writer finishes.

During the signing, Tom spots a group of twentysomethings huddled in a semicircle, all dressed stylishly in various oversized garments. Like art school kids but without the aura of entitlement and financial authority. Their sincerity is real and admirable. "They're a queer writing group," he says. "I've been emailing with the organizer." He points at the one in a dress patterned with surrealist faces, the kind I've seen in ads on Instagram.

"It's just boring writer stuff," he says. "We discuss semicolons and Twitter drama."

How much do we have to tell each other?

I watch as he introduces himself to the group. There's a lot of exclaiming. I'm happy for him; we both need more friends.

"You go," I say. "I've had a long day and still need to tinker with the painting for tomorrow."

Tom analyzes my face for subtext and finds none. I'm tired, and I have nothing exciting to say about semicolons.

THE APARTMENT IS QUIET. Somehow, it feels foreign. Tom's presence inheres in everything. All the surfaces are de facto writing desks. I pick up papers and books and place them in stacks on the table. I notice a pile of papers sheaved together on the couch: the latest draft of whatever Tom's been working on. My heart races. Should I look? I see the title, "Young Adults," in bold at the top, and begin scanning the first two paragraphs—a primal response. In them Tom is describing the first time we had sex. I notice that I'm holding my breath, but I'm also aroused.

> When I lie down on the mattress, Will picks me up and pulls me toward him. His body is large, it looms over me in an erotic way. All I want is to submit. I feel his dick stiffen against me, then he thrusts into me more gently than I deserve. It's like being filled with light.

The pleasure I feel is the pleasure of perceiving and being perceived, maybe even something like scopophilia. I masturbate on the couch, rereading the text over and over again. I feel a stinging guilt for violating Tom's privacy, but I don't stop. I put the papers down before ejaculating into a tissue.

I imagine painting the scene he describes, but the desire isn't genuine. An image would be purely pornographic, but something in Tom's writing elevates it to a more poetic dimension. It isn't just that in Tom's work we are two young men in the world and in love but that the world and love are thrumming inside us.

I don't feel upset. Truthfully, I'm thrilled to be written about, to be so clearly a subject of Tom's creative labor. I had worried that his excessive writing was indicative of a problem of attention, that I was no longer as worthy a recipient of his interest as I was in Edmonton. The essay, what I read of it, relieves me of that psychic burden. I tidy the papers and put them back where I found them.

. . .

DURING CRITIQUE, THE SEMINAR ROOM is noiseless. My body is loud by comparison, though only I can hear it. Our Practice of Art instructor, an older man named Gerald with a heavy beard and dressed entirely in gray, sits at the back, a notepad in hand. Typically he waits until the end of the critique to offer his thoughts. After a few minutes of silent contemplation, he invites questions and comments from the class.

The comments are brief and mostly complimentary. "Beautiful work," a classmate says. "It's so emotional," says another. "I understand that the painting is a tribute. You capture the beauty in the mundane powerfully."

The one straight white man in the cohort, Sam, is the last to speak: "It's a portrait, yes," he says, then pauses. "I'm sorry, but I don't see anything deeper than that. Its meaning is all at the surface. There's no depth." I think of Mulvey again: women are the *bearers of meaning, not the makers*. "I understand that as an Indigenous artist you want to present an image of an Indigenous person who isn't suffering. Is that art, though? I'd argue that that's more sociological. We're artists, not sociologists."

My jaw drops, almost cartoonishly, adrenaline coursing through me. I want to yell, to defend myself. I want to say something about aesthetic sovereignty, about how until the very recent past Indigenous art was deemed insufficiently imaginative or inventive. Indigenous artists were expected to make art about their anthropologically defined existence and nothing else. If I paint a portrait of my mother before her life changed and do so as an act of love, I am also rebelling against an interpretive history that emerged from outside our communities and limited what could be known about us. In paying homage to my mother's happiness I'm attempting to offer up a new grammar of Indigenous life. I want to say all of this with aplomb but my mouth is a flat line that leads nowhere.

"All right, that's enough," Gerald says sharply. He hasn't had to stop a student from speaking before. The atmosphere of the room is tense. We're all adults, but his tone of voice infantilizes us.

"Will," Gerald says, "I think the portrait is lovely. Maybe there's something in Sam's comments that you can reflect on, which is the difficulty of demonstrating a work's sense of purpose. I imagine the work coheres in relation to other works, past and/or future. Maybe you can make its meaning clearer."

"Thank you," I manage, pitifully.

We break before the next critique, and I gather my things and leave. It's a small insistence on freedom, an act of self-determination. I also don't want to cry in front of everyone.

I TAKE A LONGER ROUTE back to the apartment. I walk by rows of condo developments, full of people living in cramped steel boxes. Aside from the climate, the first difference between Vancouver and Edmonton that I noticed was that people on the coast had shrunk their domestic lives, adapted to the tightness. In Edmonton, in the middle of the prairies, we lived with a sense of expansiveness. My apartment, however old and unrenovated, was large; Tom and I filled it hungrily with the sounds and objects of our love. In our new place, we tiptoed around and bumped into each other. We had enough space for some plants, a table, a couch, and little else. I miss the prairies—a difficult truth to hold. I enrolled in an MFA because I wanted more time to be an artist, to defer having to consider certain economic factors. I wanted to avoid the enormity of the future. Maybe I should've soldiered on after undergrad in Edmonton, begun immediately building my body of work in my homeland. But what's two years, really? The thought clarifies something in me. I have earned myself two years to make art. I have two years to love Tom in a new city, to make future memories we'll someday cherish. I have two years to possibly fail, but if I do I also have two years to indulge in the pleasures of trying again.

. . .

AT THE APARTMENT, Tom appears to have been waiting for me to arrive. The table has been cleared of all his writerly belongings. He looks freshly showered, his hair still damp. The curtains are already parted, but the sky is overcast so only gray light seeps in. It makes the apartment feel rained in.

"How'd the critique go?"

"Oh god, terribly, but we don't have to get into it."

"Are you sure?"

I approach the table, turning on the harsh yellow light above him. It makes him look exposed and drained of vitality, which I find disturbing, but I sit down anyway.

"Yes," I say. "I want to be entirely with you right now."

Tom smiles. It's all so domestic. I want to have a domestic life. I want all our minor inconveniences to orbit around a meaningful axis. I want the petty feuds and the awkward silences. Suddenly I don't feel anxious.

"I want that too," he says. "I'm sorry I've been a little distant, always writing and working."

"Hey, it's OK," I say softly. I'm reminded of the days after my thesis show in Edmonton, how he erected a wall only he could climb over. How it was my job to be patient, to love him anyways.

"Thank you," Tom says. "I have something to tell you. If I don't say it now, I might never, and I don't want it to continue to worry me." He takes a deep breath. "I wrote an essay about our relationship, as well as some critical events right before we met. It's been accepted for publication at a small literary journal that my new writing pals told me about, published out of someone's basement. I doubt anyone's going to read it, but it feels important. I'm proud."

"That's amazing," I say. "I'd love to read it."

Tom stands up, retrieves his laptop, and places it in front of me. His hands tremble slightly.

"I should warn you that it gets graphic and very vulnerable and that you can veto anything you'd like, but you have to promise to be honest with me about how it makes you feel, OK?"

"OK."

Tom wants to write about our relationship to make us infinite.

He will look at my paintings and tell me what he thinks. I will go to his readings, and he will come to my shows. I will proofread his essays. These will be our small acts of care. We will do them time and again. Sometimes they will feel meaningless and obligatory. But we will build a shared world this way, paying attention to our lives and the art we make from them.

"All right," he says, covering his eyes with his hands. "You can read it now."

Literary Festival

AFTER SEVERAL YEARS, I had at last completed a new poetry collection. When S left, I reinvented my writing practice. I walked myself back from the cliff of creative neglect and wrote about the separation, however veiled by metaphor the subject of the poems ended up being. I wrote furiously and with emotional abandon. I wanted to admit to everything I did wrong so that I could become someone new. In the marketing copy my publisher described the collection as "a finely wrought meditation on the joy and agony of a lived life." I wasn't sure if I was supposed to see this as an objective truth or as a necessary lie I'd chosen to be in on. I knew that my creative process was neither neat nor entirely purposeful. I wrote deep into the night during bouts of depression. I wrote because it was a way of living that didn't flatten the intensity of my sadness. I wrote because there was little else I wanted to do with my spare time between sleeping and teaching. The book received minimal attention, which was fine; I was used to it. *Poetry is one of the few historically minor forms*—I said this to my students every semester—*and therein lies its political possibility.* I was working hard to firmly believe this myself.

I had been invited to just one literary festival, held in a small city in the middle of the prairies. I'd never been before, nor had anyone I knew. They couldn't pay me much beyond a small honorarium, but I didn't care. All I knew about the city was its fraught history, being a site of state-sanctioned racism throughout most of the twentieth century—it was for many decades an outpost of rural white animosity, embroiled in scandals of indentured labor. The festival director promised that I would be part of a "lively and engaging" panel with an audience of "book lovers" who rarely had the opportunity to be in conversation with "esteemed authors." I understood that this language was intended to be more than descriptive or anticipatory; it was intended to bring something into being, to impose a reality. This wasn't exactly morally suspect, as this was the way poets used language too. I wrote about the future because I wanted to invent it. I wrote about the present so that it wouldn't obliterate me.

·   ·   ·

ON THE AIRPLANE, I read a new book by a self-described postmodernist comprised entirely of random observations. Sometimes it was interesting, but mostly it was unruly and without purpose. I appreciated the aesthetic power of the purposeless, especially in contrast to the self-helpification of literature, but about halfway through it struck me that it was a gimmick only certain writers, mostly white men, could get away with. I put the book down on my lap and glanced over at the man sitting beside me. I wondered what his random thoughts were, what he'd title the book in which they were compiled. Throughout the entire two-hour flight, he scrolled through the camera roll on his phone. I thought I saw him swipe past a couple dick pics.

Despite being so high in the sky, I didn't feel any closer to heaven. As a teen, I assumed being closer to heaven was the whole point of air travel. As an adult, when I flew, I felt over-determined by my fragility, as though I needed to be protected, which incidentally might have something to do with the allure of heaven.

We descended as I was nearing the end of the book, which I'd started to look at rather than read. I was stunned anew by the vastness of the prairie landscape—it didn't matter how many times I'd seen a city burst out of an expanse of green from several thousand feet above. I didn't feel like God; I felt like a lonely man. The scene was a beautiful and terrible thing to behold. The landscape, sliced up according to agricultural desires, was unlike a poem because it required an ongoing violence to function (poems could be put to violent use, of course, but a poem was seldom intrinsically violent). Some prairie cities were once a fort or a fur-trading post. Some prairie cities were frontiers, harbingers of native suffering. It felt as though I was plummeting directly into this difficult history.

A FESTIVAL ORGANIZER greeted me in the arrivals lounge. Her name was Rachel and she identified herself as "The Poetry Lady." She said she was in charge of all poetry-related happenings in the small city to which we were now headed. Without prompt, she described her long-standing affinity with poetry, beginning in high school when she was entranced by Shakespeare's *Sonnets*. I confessed I had read only Shakespeare's tragic plays, and only because it was mandatory in an English class. She quipped that that was its own tragedy. I looked out the window at the flat landscape, which made everything visible;

I could see cattle near the horizon. Rachel, too, was splaying herself out like a landscape. I resisted saying too much about myself. The autobiographical suddenly felt like a foreign mode. I recognized that this was a fault of mine and not Rachel's. I wanted to protect something but couldn't decipher what. I thought of the Louise Glück lines: "It was a time / governed by contradictions, as in / I felt nothing and / I was afraid." In the passenger seat of Rachel's car, I felt nothing and I was afraid. I felt afraid and I was nothing.

"I've read all your books, by the way," she said. "I had to hunt for the first two—they're out of print. How unfortunate. The first is my favorite."

I published that book in my twenties. It was about first love. The book felt distant now. I rarely thought about it, nor did I ever read from it at events. I was embarrassed by my publishing life— which was different from my writing life—as I was ultimately an insignificant figure, one whose books went out of print without fanfare. Maybe it wasn't just embarrassment, but also self-love, insofar as I had to love myself enough to want to be different. I had an urge to get out of the car, to be among the cattle, whose indifference I knew I would surely mistake for sympathy.

"What are you working on?" I asked.

"Oh, you know, a bit of everything. A poetry collection, a memoir."

"What's the memoir about? If you don't mind my asking."

"Alas, I'm one of those superstitious types," she said. "Can't speak about a writing project until it's done."

I couldn't relate. My work was best when it was unfinished, when it was still partly abstract, when it could become anything.

"I can respect that," I said.

The car seemed tinier. I suddenly became aware of my large-ness. My knees were pressing against the glove compartment, my shoulder kept bumping the side window. Was Rachel's driving erratic or was I imagining it? Why hadn't I rented a car? I had to remind myself that Rachel was a good person.

I dissociated the rest of the drive and was dropped off in front of a casino hotel. The city was as unremarkable as I had envisioned it. I thought there would be more Indigenous folks, but the only people I saw on the streets were white. Something about it was stuck in the previous century, from the architecture to the general atmosphere of white kinship. I hurried into the hotel lobby, where I had to insist to the receptionist that my room had been covered by the festival. After several minutes and a phone call with a superior, I was given a key card. My room was on the top floor, next to the elevator. The room itself hadn't been updated in decades, the TV looked like a relic of another time, and the heavy fabric curtains were not only ugly but also exuded a stale smell. I took a moment to suppress my middle-class panic and lay down on the bed.

The festival didn't start until the next morning. I began to miss S, who always made me go sightseeing when we first arrived in a new city. It was in my nature to remain in as private a space as possible, so I resolved that I would simply stay in the room for the remainder of the day.

IN THE HOTEL, I truly began to feel like nothing. I tried to read one of the many books I had packed but I had a headache and my concentration waned. I entertained the idea of leaving, of booking a flight home or anywhere else. I could disappear; no one would miss a minor poet. I went as far as pulling up the flight options. I could catch a red-eye, there was a shuttle that could take me to the airport, I hadn't unpacked yet. I closed the browser and ran a bath instead. In the tub, I tried to reckon with my existential unraveling, but I was also naked and thus couldn't bring the necessary seriousness to the task. The tub was small and the water kept seeping into the overflow drain. I could hear the elevator going up and down, up and down. People's conversations carried into the bathroom. All I could hear were scraps of language.

A poet unraveling in a bathtub—had I become a cliché? It wasn't the first time this had occurred to me. What was the relationship between hotel rooms and depression? Why did I always feel so feral in one, less like a citizen of the earth? When I got out and dried off and put on underwear, I tried to write at the small desk. Maybe I could conduct my own postmodernist experiment of total self-representation. I started to recount the day's proceedings, from the time I woke up to the car ride with Rachel, but it felt like an indictment of my character. I stopped writing and reread all the poems in my new book. Tomorrow would be the first time I read them aloud for an audience. I wasn't sure I would write another book. When was a writer finished? Did I know how to stop?

I had a nap and woke up sweaty and starving. The air-conditioning had shut off, apparently a power-saving measure. I ordered room service and ate a burger greedily. My stomach lurched in protest, urging me to slow down, but I didn't. I opened the window and heard the murmur of street conversation. I tinkered with some draft poems and for the first time that day felt a small burst of life inside me. I kept writing.

I WOKE UP in the middle of the night and was afraid again. It sounded as though someone were trying to get into the room. I tiptoed over to the door and peeked through the peephole—nothing. Awake, I lay back down and opened Tinder, swiping through the array of men, most of whom were too young; I matched with a few but didn't dig any deeper into their profiles. Instead, I combed through my emails. I'd missed one from Rachel, inviting me to dinner with the other authors—fuck. She'd sent a follow-up a few hours later checking to see if I was all right. Maybe she noticed that I was agitated in the car. I deleted the emails without responding and lay in the dark for a couple hours, thinking about the humid earth.

.   .   .

MY PANEL, MYSTERIOUSLY CALLED "POETIC POTIONS," was the first of the day. I surveyed the room and found that most of the attendees were invited authors. I recognized only two of them, both commercially successful novelists. After opening remarks from the festival organizers, several people left the conference room; then my panel started. A few more people wandered in. I'd wondered who the other poet on the panel would be, but it turned out he missed his flight. Part of me envied him. The director said I could take up the entire hour if I wanted. I couldn't tell if she actually wanted me to. I took to the podium and stared at the small audience. Everyone looked back with ambivalence.

"It's lovely to be here," I said. "I'm going to read some poems, then talk about my process." I read from a poem that was made up of fragments I had saved from discarded poems:

> *In a stranger's lap, I was a toppled*
> *statue. Really, I wanted to be as free*
> *as the middle of a late spring. After all,*
> *I was a boy playing in the ditch*
> *of history.*

Then another from a recent project:

It is a summer afternoon and the sun
is obsessed with me. All my friends
text me bad news. We can't escape the past,
we fall in love too easily, we talk about the wars—
the one against natives, the one overseas.

When I finished, people murmured their support. A young person snapped his fingers. From my tote bag, I pulled out a notepad onto which I'd jotted some thoughts that morning at the hotel.

I cleared my throat. "Poetry is a literary activity, but it can also be understood as the way people creatively resist colonial-capitalist enclosure," I said. I felt a couple audience members tune out at the mention of "colonial-capitalist enclosure." Some people thought those kinds of words were meaningless, too large to shape real life. "It is vital to me that we defend this other notion of poetry so as to ensure poems aren't simply a method of self-reflection but also tools for collective struggle." Fueled by the one young person nodding vigorously, I began adlibbing. It wasn't unlike teaching, I thought, trying to demonstrate a way of thinking rather than just expressing some views that could be assessed as true or false; ultimately, your goal was to affect someone's way of thinking. I imagined the two audience members resisted my way of thinking all the same. I felt sad for them, as I sometimes did for my more conservative students, who by the close of a term of studying political poetry had only solidified their prior ideologies, but my sadness meant nothing in the end, as it also didn't now.

I finished fifteen minutes early. No one had any questions,

which was a relief. As the small group filtered out of the room, I noticed I had a Tinder message from someone named Luke.

"Great talk!" it read.

I looked around the lobby and saw him waving—it was the man who'd been snapping during my talk. I approached.

"Luke?"

"That's me."

He appeared to be about the age of my students. He was tall, slim. His shirt was tucked into a pair of chinos. I could see that his hair was blond and wavy under a hat.

"Thanks for coming."

"My pleasure. I love your work."

"That's very kind of you," I said, glancing at the time.

"Oh, are you off?"

"No, no, just thinking I should grab coffee before the next panel."

"Can I join?"

"I don't see why not," I said.

As we walked to the café, Luke told me he was an aspiring writer. He was doing an internship with a local literary organization and had urged the festival organizers to extend the invite to me.

"I was surprised when we matched on Tinder," Luke said when conversation lulled.

I felt embarrassed, unprofessional. "Ah yes, what's with this new rhetoric of intimacy anyways? Is it changing how we understand our desires?" I said, trying to intellectualize our exchange, keep it away from the erotic.

"I've grown up with it. That language has always been my language," he said.

"Well, not me. I remember using an entirely different code. Stolen glances, furtive touches."

"That'd be a good name for a book," he said. I detested writers trying to turn everything into a book title. I chuckled anyways.

We ordered coffee; I bought his. He continued to tell me about the book he was trying to write, the MFA programs he was thinking of applying to.

"If you need advice, let me know," I said. "I'd be happy to lend an eye."

"I'll hold you to that," he said, jotting down my email address. I felt immediate regret.

"By the way," he said, this time in a lower register, "there's a private bathroom down the hall." Luke nodded toward the back of the café. "What do you think?"

I was surprised to be solicited so publicly. Luke was the sort of attractive that empowered this kind of brazen confidence. Men likely orbited around him with sexual interest all the time. I couldn't stop thinking about how different we were, how I never assumed anyone wanted to fuck me. "Sorry," I managed after a pause, "but I really do need to run."

"Oh, of course," he said. "Hey, don't be a stranger. I'm around all day. I'll see you at the festival, I'm sure."

I left the café in a rush and walked to the hotel, deciding not to return to the venue after all.

LATER I RECEIVED AN EMAIL from my publicist. Rachel had reached out to him to express concern over my having missed the welcome dinner and not sticking around after my panel to sign books or mingle. People were disappointed. There was another dinner tonight, and I was expected to be there. My publicist said he didn't want to be pushy but thought I should participate, save face, make amends. I didn't respond. Instead, I napped for a few hours.

FROM OUTSIDE THE RESTAURANT, I could see the group of invited authors and festival staff at a table near the back. Everyone was laughing. It was late evening but the sun was still oppressively warm, making me clammy underneath a heavy blazer.

"Sorry I'm late," I said, sitting next to one of the commercial novelists.

"We were worried about you," the director said. "I was going to send someone over."

Everyone looked at me with the kind of pity reserved for the downtrodden or the recently widowed.

"I don't mean to be evasive," I said. "I'm OK, but I appreciate the concern."

The group resumed their conversations. I tried to take part but my one-liners floundered. I had already marked myself as an outsider, someone uninterested in assimilating to a circumstantial group dynamic. Eventually the commercial novelist turned to me.

"I don't usually do these smaller festivals," he said in a hushed voice, "but the director is an old family friend. My mother insisted. She'd been getting persistent emails."

"They are persistent, aren't they?" We laughed.

"Sorry I missed your talk, I had a call with my agent. We're selling the film rights to one of my novels—it's chaos."

"Good chaos though, no?"

He paused. "Yes, of course, of course, but I'm still losing sleep over it. One production company is promising all kinds of things, another is more critically acclaimed but their budget is low."

"So, the decision is between more money or a more inter-esting film?"

"Essentially, yes. What would you do?"

The answer was obvious to me. "I'd go with the more artful company. I'd want the film to be meaningful."

"I'd expect that much from a poet," he said coyly. We laughed again, though I understood I was the joke we were in on. "I've never met a poet who could live off his books," he added. "What a shame."

I didn't tell him that I never wanted to "live off" my poems. Rather my poems enabled me to keep living. It sounded silly, but I told this to my students constantly anyways. I wondered if his novels kept him alive in this sense.

As everyone parted ways, Rachel pulled me aside.

"I'm glad you joined us," she said.

"It was my pleasure," I said as earnestly as I could.

"It's OK if it wasn't." She winked. "Safe travels tomorrow."

After she left, I stood in the same spot for a few minutes, illuminated by a flickering sign that said "TAKE-OUT." Everything was tinged with the surreal. I knew I wouldn't see her again, that I wouldn't be invited back. My sadness made the world seem both enormous and puny; what little I had that was mine still felt smothering and heavy. I wanted to put my life down on the street and walk away.

AT THE HOTEL, I got into bed without taking my clothes off. I fantasized about becoming a recluse, leaving public life. Then I thought about wanting to die—it was a desire so urgent I had to name it, if even just in my head.

A knock at the door. I tried to ignore it, but it persisted. I walked over, looked through the peephole—it was Luke. His presence was unexpected. Remembering the earlier interaction, I felt annoyed.

"I can tell you're at the door," he said.

"How did you know where I was staying?"

"The receptionist told me. I said I was with the festival."

Yikes, I thought. "You could've messaged me."

"I tried—a lot."

I rested my head against the door, unsure what to say.

"I wanted to apologize for earlier," he added. "I think I misunderstood what was happening. Maybe we could grab a drink? I didn't get to ask you some of the writerly questions I had."

I didn't respond.

"Can you open the door at least? I can come in."

"I think that's a bad idea," I said.

I heard him pacing.

"Well, fuck you too, man," he said half-heartedly, with no malice at all. It was tender in a way.

I heard him step into the elevator. When he was gone, I put my back against the door, then slid down to the ground.

It was as if I were in a poem I couldn't figure out how to finish. I was in the thick of my own disintegrating narrative existence. I tried to will myself to cry, but nothing happened. I opened my phone, saw the stream of messages from Luke and considered calling him, apologizing and letting him inside after all. Instead I threw my phone under the bed and heard it ricochet against the wall. I closed my eyes and felt that I'd become a part of the hotel room, an inanimate object, a furnishing. If I wasn't a poet, the feeling might've destroyed me.

Outside

JACK'S TRIAL CAME SOONER than expected, and, because of the pandemic, it was held online. "Thank fuck my lawyer knew what he was doing, because I didn't," he later said, to anyone who'd listen. The drug trafficking charges were dropped due to missing evidence—Jack couldn't remember the precise details. In the end, he was charged with possession and put on probation. It seemed like a miracle. His kokum, Mary, cried on the video call, the only relative of Jack's in attendance. Everyone heard her; she hadn't turned off her mic. Jack was relieved she was crying because it meant he didn't have to.

The next day Mary picked him up from the Remand Centre even though she despised driving in the city. His license had been revoked, but he took over once they left the city limits. He didn't worry about getting stopped and thrown back in jail; his freedom, however new, made him feel invincible in a way he hadn't felt since childhood. He was defiant like a small boy ignoring rules he didn't believe in, hurtling back toward northern Alberta with the windows all the way down. The relentless wind in his face told a story he couldn't find the language for.

Jack pulled into a McDonald's drive-thru and ordered more food than he could eat alone, and Mary nibbled on the leftovers. She was busy lecturing him. She told him that he had to change his life, that she wouldn't be around that much longer, which meant he wouldn't have someone to retrieve him from jail when he made mistakes. She was always reminding him that she would soon pass on—she was nearing eighty. He knew when she did no one else would care about him; he hated that prospect as much as she did. Something in him resisted the fact of her age. He wanted her to live forever, or at least as long as he did. Despite everything, the world still made absolute sense with her in it with him.

· · ·

BACK ON THE RESERVE, Jack moved into a small trailer across from the Band Office, the building where Chief and Council meet. They welcomed Jack back sincerely but also wanted to make it more difficult for him to sell again under their watchful eyes. Chief and Council held a great deal of power on the reserve—they could grant the cops search warrants if necessary. It did occur to Jack to start selling again, mostly because it was easy to settle back into, to make money from, but the thought of the hurt it'd cause Mary was enough, for now, to keep him from doing so.

When he first opened the door to the trailer, he gasped. "It smells musty as fuck," he said to Mary, who winced at the coarse language. The walls were stained with indiscernible liquids of varying shades of brown. The window in the main bedroom had been smashed with a rock that still sat in the middle of the room. The stove had been pulled away from the wall and left near the back door; someone had tried to steal it and given up. He went with Mary back to her house to get cleaning supplies and an old couch from the basement that he'd once used as a bed. He didn't like being back there because it reminded him of the arrest, his subsequent jail time, and all the anguish it brought Mary. At his insistence, they left as soon as possible. That night, exhausted from cleaning and from the drive north, Jack fell asleep on the couch in the clothes he'd been wearing since his release. He'd forgotten to turn the lights off.

Throughout the following week, Jack and Mary continued to tidy up the trailer and the yard. It was hard work. Mary did more than her body could handle, but she never complained. Every evening, Mary cooked. Jack didn't know how to and never had to learn. Most mornings, he made do with coffee and toast. He didn't have much of an appetite anyways, had adjusted to eating small portions. Prison took a lot from a person.

• • •

ON FRIDAY JACK MET WITH his probation officer at the trailer for the first time. The officer came by in a mask and gloves, and when he stepped inside he looked surprised that everything was tidy and in order. He was a new hire, and Jack didn't recognize him. The blue nonmedical mask framed his face such that he looked severe, unfriendly.

"Looking for a job?"

"Not yet."

"Why not?"

"The pandemic."

"Who's helping you tidy the place?"

"My kokum."

"What's her name?"

"Mary."

"What does she do?"

"For work?"

"Yes."

"She's retired."

"No drugs?"

"No sir."

"Alcohol?"

"Not a drop."

"How does it feel?"

"What?"

"To be sober."

"I don't think about it." (A lie.)

The officer didn't write any of this down, just looked Jack in the eyes. After he left, Jack felt as though he were still being watched. He called Mary to see if she wanted to drive into town, but she had visitors over for a socially distanced coffee. He decided to walk to her house. It was the middle of a work-day, but the Band Office and the handful of businesses were mostly empty. People were working from home or not at all. There were more kids out than adults. Several drove by Jack on quads. "Hey, I thought you were in jail," one yelled. Jack ignored him, kept walking. The convenience store was still open, so Jack thought about buying cigarettes, but he didn't have enough cash on him. When he turned off the highway and onto the dirt road that led to Mary's house, he saw the police detach-ment in the distance. A few cruisers were parked outside. He thought about native police officers locking up native men. He was angry and sad. He thought about the men he'd befriended in jail, all from reserves in northern Alberta. He wondered if they were outside yet. He missed some of them, which he wasn't prepared for. Inside, they formed a community. All they had was one another.

. . .

THE NEXT WEEK, while rummaging through his old room at Mary's, Jack found an iPad he'd received as payment for weed a while back. After charging it he downloaded Tinder. Mary had just gotten wireless internet. The connection was spotty, but it would suffice. He needed a profile picture, so he took a selfie in the bathroom in his jeans and hoodie. The photo was blurry, but he used it anyways. The settings showed women as far south as Edmonton, but that was impractical—he couldn't drive. He narrowed the distance to the span of the lake, an approximately fifty-mile range. He swiped right on everyone who wasn't his cousin, then waited. Dating someone felt urgent to him insofar as being on his own, especially on the outside, ratcheted up his more self-destructive urges. Alone most nights, his self was a rolling river he had to try to enclose. At worst, it was a terrible nature he wanted to at last be free from. He believed a partner, a woman who could put up with him, would make his inner world less loud and unpredictable.

That night, Jack managed to connect to the Band Office's Wi-Fi, and so he opened Tinder again. He came across a woman he'd gone to high school with. Her name was Lucy and she was living just down the road in a duplex with her cousins. She looked beautiful. In each of her photos, she was smiling, the sun behind her. Jack hadn't seen her in ages. He remembered that she was quiet and well-liked, that they belonged to different social circles and hadn't managed an entire conversation. Jack assumed she wouldn't entertain his advances, but he held on to hope. He thought about the most recent woman he'd dated—he hadn't treated her with the care she deserved. He often left her messages unanswered, even had a brief affair with someone in their friend group. This was just a few weeks before he was jailed. He wanted to be different. Scrolling through Lucy's photos again, he was afraid, both of himself and of rejection. He didn't know how people changed. Mary made it sound so simple, as though he could wake up any morning and have transformed overnight. She needed to hold on to that fantasy in order to love Jack and not unravel. Jack lived indeterminately in Mary's utopian vision; he had nowhere else to go. It was his motherland.

The iPad buzzed. He and Lucy had matched. Without hesitation, he sent her a message.

"How r u?"

The message was read instantly. *Fuck*, he thought. *Should I have used an emoji?*

"I'm OK, thank you," she wrote. "So, you're back on the rez, eh?"

"I guess so aha."

"I heard you were in jail."

He put the device down. *Of course she knew, everyone gossips, talks shit.*

Eventually he wrote, "I was. Cops had it out for me." It was something like the truth.

"They really don't let any of us live," Lucy replied. "Not sure why they built the new detachment. I couldn't believe it when they put syllabics up. That's our language, not the colonizer's."

Jack read the message a few times. He didn't entirely follow, couldn't remember what syllabics were. He'd seen the symbols on the detachment but hadn't thought much of them. No one had taught him anything about his ancestral language.

"The rez cops are colonizers? Aha even Greg?" Greg was

an older native guy who'd been transferred to the reserve a few years ago from farther north. Generally, he let people be.

"Basically XD."

"That's funny as hell."

Jack learned that Lucy was also unemployed after being temporarily let go from her job at a café. The owner promised she'd be hired back once the virus settled. There weren't currently any active cases in northern Alberta, Lucy explained. She tracked the numbers, watched the televised updates from Edmonton. She'd texted the café owner, but so far received no response. She was bored, impatient. At least she was getting the COVID money, she conceded. It was the most money she'd ever had in her bank account.

"We should hang out," Jack said at last.

After several minutes, the app showed that she still hadn't read the message.

He typed "Or not." Then deleted it. "Fuck you then." Also deleted. He tried the calming techniques he'd been taught inside: breathing into his feet, then out into the universe. He never understood what that meant, but he tried anyways. It seemed to work. He felt less anxious. He closed the app and went outside, leaving the iPad on the couch.

WALKING, JACK SPOTTED A TEEN he used to sell drugs to, some kid with extra money. He was standing on the other side of the highway, so he looked small, thinner than Jack remembered. He waved, but Jack didn't wave back, so the kid gave him the finger. He looked miserable, which made Jack feel winded with a kind of vertigo. Somehow he hadn't thought about the people whose lives he'd messed with when he was a dealer. The desire to smoke something—a joint, a cigarette—was powerful in him. He decided he'd smoke a cigarette when he got home. For now, he would lie down in the grass in front of the Band Office. A truck passed while he lay there stoically. "You OK?" came a disembodied voice. Jack waved him away.

THE SUN HADN'T QUITE SET when he got back to the trailer. Orange light trickled into the living area.

He grabbed the iPad—a message from Lucy.

"I'd like to *get to know you.* Not hangout, not mess around. That clear?" She'd written about ten minutes ago.

"Yes, ma'am," Jack wrote hastily.

He wasn't sure what to do with all his feelings. Instead of sitting with them, he dug around for a cigarette and lit it on the stovetop burner (a "traditional teaching"). He opened the bedroom window, which he'd just replaced, sticking his head out to smoke. In the patch of forest across the road, there were two deer grazing, a stag and a doe. Jack watched them in awe, took in their grace and vulnerability as though they were good omens sent personally to him. They were two reasons to live, two reasons to believe he could defy the odds history had stacked against him.

LUCY INVITED HIM TO A FAMILY BARBECUE on the weekend. Jack almost didn't go. He didn't want to meet her entire family so soon. "We've already met," Lucy reminded him via text. "We're not strangers." It was the rez way. First or second or third date, it didn't really matter; you integrated into your lover's family web without pomp. Jack walked to her auntie's house behind the convenience store. Lucy saw him approach and waved him over. She was wearing a dress that swayed in the wind and made her look ethereal. Jack was nervous. He wanted desperately to be good enough for her.

She grabbed his hand and pulled him toward the small crowd, introducing him to her uncles and aunties, her cousins and grandparents. No one seemed overly interested in him, which he appreciated. He sat in a lawn chair beside Lucy. They didn't talk much, but they didn't have to. They were holding hands, sharing a single current of affection. Jack laughed at her jokes, watched her interact with her family, play with her cousin's baby, beaming inside the whole time. No one asked about his time in the Remand Centre. Lucy had an uncle who'd been jailed before, he remembered, so being in jail wasn't a shock or a disgrace—it was something that sometimes happened to people you loved. This freed him a little.

In the evening, Jack and Lucy lay on the trampoline behind the house, carving out a microcosm of pseudo-privacy like teenagers. Lucy's cousins had moved to the basement to play video games. The uncles and aunties had left for radio bingo or to watch *Wheel of Fortune*. They could at last talk to each other.

"So, tell me about your life," Lucy said.

"Fuck," Jack said. "It ain't that easy." He was looking at a crow swooping between two massive spruce trees.

"Hey," she said, elbowing him gently. "I'm not going to judge you or anything."

Jack had only been at the party for two hours, but he already trusted her.

"Well, I was raised by my kokum because my parents were too young," he said. "Got bored with school even though I was good at it. Got into drugs, dropped out, started selling, got arrested. Now I'm here." It was a pretty short story after all. He grimaced.

Lucy looked up. In the distance, an eagle circled.

"Oh god, I'm sorry, but how native is it that there's an eagle over there."

They burst into laughter.

"Well, how's your life been?" he asked.

"Simpler," she said. "Graduated, went to college for a bit, didn't like it, too much stress, came back to the rez. I moved in with my cousins because I couldn't stand to be back with my parents. I would've felt like a failure."

They continued on this way, revealing as much of their inner worlds and personal histories as possible. They each recognized that they needed to arrive as close to the present as they could in order to move forward.

As dusk approached, they walked back to Lucy's place, where she invited Jack in. The house was empty tonight.

"I want to kiss you," she said, inching toward him at the door.

"Are you sure?"

"Yes," she said, pulling Jack toward her.

When they kissed Jack felt truly *outside*. Inside, outside, these were now the terms that shaped his reality. One could be outside but still inside. Lucy was his new outside. It was terrifying and glorious how firmly Jack believed this.

Despite their agreement to move slowly, they had sex that night. It confirmed that what was between them was true and alive. In the following weeks, they met up often, alternating between houses. Jack's old and rundown trailer became imbued with life. Mary welcomed Lucy into their little world with the gratefulness of a long-suffering grandmother. Neither Jack nor Lucy counted the days since their initial meeting— their time together exceeded what they knew about romantic convention. In the minds of some, nosy neighbors and relatives, they moved too fast, but to Jack he had already had so much time stolen from him, months and months eroded away in the Remand Centre, that he made use of a different vocabulary of intimacy. His desperation was that of someone whose fate had suddenly shifted away from prolonged loss. And so all their subtle gestures of affection and care, both in and out of the bedroom, in private and in public, were how they declared their love before they were able to actually say it. True love, they each thought in their own idiosyncratic way, is in the air; it resides in objects as well as in time itself. The past seemed to almost dissolve in response, which is to say Jack no longer agonized about the arrest. Lucy's love opened space inside his mind for different memories. That was how love changed people: it made you want to give yourself over to new pasts, to future emotional histories. It made you ache to be alive.

TIME CONTINUED TO UNWIND SWIFTLY, something Jack hadn't thought was possible anymore. For a while, he had thought he'd be stuck in jail time for the rest of his life. If nothing else, Lucy had spared him that.

Because the pandemic raged on, Jack and Lucy spent most of their days together. It was now the fall. Ultimately, they didn't "date"; they became a couple. Nothing needed to be negotiated or spelled out.

Every Friday, Lucy sat in on Jack's visits with the probation officer, making sure he didn't do anything illegal or degrading. She studied the laws, knew them by heart. Jack was so impressed he thought she should become a lawyer, but he was too scared of her leaving to suggest it. Mary adored her, had recently started calling her "my girl." When she looked at Lucy and Jack sometimes she teared up. Jack felt that he'd finally made her proud, confirmed that her hope was worth something.

Jack and Lucy began a routine of waking up early to go running. Jack stopped smoking and started eating better. Lucy wanted to lose weight, which Jack thought was silly, but he supported her anyways. Jack had started working out in the Remand Centre, so he slipped into the exercise regime with ease. He became Lucy's personal trainer, and he liked being of use to her in this small way, feeling that he owed her a whole lifetime of care.

One Friday morning Lucy woke up with painful cramps and opted to stay in bed, insisting that Jack carry on as planned. The sun was already beating down hard when he took off running along a dirt road. He couldn't help but worry about Lucy. After a mile he turned around and sprinted back, arriving at the trailer sweaty and panting.

Lucy was hunched in a ball on the couch. "Painkillers aren't helping," she said. Jack hadn't seen her in this much distress before.

"What are you feeling?"

Lucy hesitated. "Pain all over my pelvis, stomach. If it's PMS, the cramps have never been this brutal."

"Do you want to go the hospital?"

"Jack, it's Friday," she said.

His stomach dropped. "Oh fuck, right."

The probation officer would arrive at the same time he always did, in just a few hours. Jack couldn't risk missing the appointment; they would issue a warrant in a heartbeat. What's more, the hospital was overrun these days. Case numbers had climbed. Doctors were leaving, either to retire or to transfer out of rural medicine. Lucy could be in the waiting room all day. Jack hated the idea of her alone in the hospital but understood she shouldn't have to bear the pain needlessly.

"I'll go, you stay," she said assertively. "I'll call one of my cousins to drive me."

After a few attempts a cousin at last answered and agreed to pick her up if she paid for gas. Jack kissed her on the forehead in relief, which made her wince, her body on edge.

"Ugh, you're so sweaty," she said after composing herself. Her teasing was a joy—it kept Jack from crumbling.

ABOUT AN HOUR LATER, when Lucy had already arrived at the hospital in town, Jack received a call from the probation officer.

"Sorry to do this to you man, but I'm not going to be able to make it to the reserve today. You'll have to come to the court-house in town."

"What if I don't have a ride?" Jack asked, already furious.

"You'll have to figure it out. The rules of your probation are very clear." A pause. "Sorry, Jack, I have to run. I'll see you in a couple hours."

Jack called Mary, but she wasn't answering her landline, which she still relied on. She rarely used the cellphone she'd been recently gifted by Lucy and Jack. He had no one else to call, no one he wanted to be indebted to.

Without forethought, he gathered his phone and wallet and headed outside. He would hitchhike. For a few minutes, he stood on the corner where the highway and the road to the convenience store met. A handful of cars drove by. No one looked at him. He stuck his thumb out, as he'd seen countless people do before. As motorists continued to pass by, he started walking. At first, he was on the shoulder of the highway, but some vehicles came too close, so he moved into the ditch, stepping over trash and animal carcasses. That didn't last long; it occurred to him he wouldn't get a ride from anyone if he were in the ditch. People would think the worst.

He tried calling Mary again—no answer. *Where the fuck is she?* A familiar wave of rage welled up inside him.

His mouth became dry with thirst. He glanced over at the forest; the trees were mostly leafless. Their aura was foreboding, so much so that Jack felt that if he were to enter the forest he might never leave it. He checked the time. He had an hour and a half. He'd need at least a short ride from someone to make the appointment, so he jumped back onto the highway. Several logging trucks passed, generating a wind that almost knocked him over. Eventually he crossed the train tracks into a small hamlet. There was a wide shoulder ahead that truck drivers often used as a rest stop; from afar, he saw a few vehicles parked. Jack jogged and approached a man who'd just finished peeing.

"Sorry, man, I ain't got nothing for you," he said, before scrambling into his car.

Another man, upon seeing the interaction, shut the hood of his truck and got inside.

Someone pulled up beside Jack. It was a native lady he didn't recognize, from a different rez. "Hey, everything OK?" she asked through a slight opening in the passenger-side window.

"I'm trying to get to town. Are you heading that way?" Jack hoped he didn't sound as deranged as he felt.

"I can give you a ride as far as the next rez." That would save him about fifteen miles. He jumped inside.

They were silent most of the drive, country music playing loudly on the radio.

"Ain't right what they did," the woman said at last. "Those guys, ignoring you, assuming the worst."

"It's whatever," he said. "I'm used to it."

"Don't mean it's right."

Jack wasn't sure what to say, so he said nothing.

The woman didn't have the air-conditioning on, and it was getting uncomfortably hot in the car. Jack rolled down the window.

"Please don't," she said, eyes still on the highway.

The woman let Jack out at a gas station. He figured he could make it in time without another ride if he ran. At first, his pace was fast, faster than he ever moved during a routine run. Then he started to feel light-headed and slowed down to a light jog. He was struggling to stay within the shoulder and kept veering too close to the road. As he was trying to correct his balance he tripped and tumbled into the ditch, rolling over a few times. He laid still for a few minutes. *Is this how everything gets fucked up?* His phone was no longer in his pocket. *Fuck, fuck, fuck.* He sat up and scanned the area—nothing. He thought about lying back down and never moving again. The grass around him was already dying, coarse under his touch. *No*, he thought, *I have to keep moving.*

He stood up, dizzy, and stuck his thumb out again. He walked for what felt like thirty minutes, but he couldn't be certain. All he knew was that he was running out of time.

Then, as he was losing faith, Mary pulled over just ahead of him and honked. Jack thought he was hallucinating, but he could hear her shouting his name. He ran over.

"Get in," she said. Her tone was familiar—stern but empathetic. He'd heard it many times. It meant she was disappointed in him but loved him enough not to say it directly.

"I think you just saved my life," he said.

JACK AND MARY arrived at the courthouse five minutes before the appointment. Jack cleaned up as best he could with McDonald's napkins from Mary's glove compartment. He had grass stains on his pants and his hands were blistered. For the first time since leaving jail, he felt as feral as the correctional officers thought he was. Inside, the probation officer was waiting in the lobby and handed him a mask.

"Didn't think you were going to make it," he said. "I thought it was going to be a sad day for you."

He gestured toward an office, and Jack complied wordlessly. The conversation went as it always did. It was over in fifteen minutes. Jack was both relieved and enraged. The officer toyed with Jack's life, demonstrated how much power he held over him. He would've tossed Jack back in jail without a second thought. Jack had been made puny and destructible—the goal of carceral punishment. He closed his eyes and breathed into his feet. He thought about Lucy, about their life together, then got up and left.

THE HOSPITAL WAS CROWDED. People were coughing, sneezing. Others were on stretchers in the hallways, seemingly lifeless. Jack scanned the faces for Lucy, but she wasn't among them. He asked a nurse if she could help, but without meeting his gaze she said he had to register at the desk first. Jack rang the bell on the counter. He didn't care if he appeared aggressive, which he tried to avoid when seeking medical attention. Finally a nurse appeared, looking annoyed. Jack told her about Lucy, and she skimmed through a pile of charts.

"You're the boyfriend?" she asked skeptically.

"Yes."

She glanced at the chart again. "She's in the room at the end of the hall." Jack jogged over and pushed open the door. He felt as though they'd been apart for days. She was sitting in a chair in a pale blue hospital gown, her cousin beside her. A doctor sat across from them, typing at a computer. The sight of her made him want to collapse. He could reorient himself in his life, his body.

"Jack," she said, "I'm pregnant."

MARY DROVE JACK AND LUCY BACK to the reserve. In the back seat, Lucy rested her head on Jack. She said, "I want to have this baby." Jack couldn't manage a response. She fell asleep waiting for one.

Mary kept glancing at Jack in the rearview mirror. He couldn't tell what she was trying to communicate, but he thought he saw tears in her eyes. Eventually, he dozed off too.

At the trailer, Jack carried Lucy inside and into the bedroom. The medication to ease the nausea had made her drowsy. She continued sleeping as he placed her onto the mattress. He opened a window and closed the door behind him.

It was late afternoon. There was still so much of the day left.

Jack felt an urge to run away, to leave everything behind, to reinvent himself and find some other rez to haunt.

What he knew about native fatherhood was colored by his own experience of paternal abandonment. He grew up inundated with unfulfilled promises. For a little boy, the world is nothing but a series of promises, kept and unkept. To be fatherless was akin to being worldless. Jack wanted to build a family, yes. This longing, however abstract until now, was obvious, but he was scared that he'd replicate that experience of slow agony for his own child. All he knew about being a decent father was speculation, secondhand stories. It felt like a fuzzy dream he'd have to somehow make real. No blueprint was codified inside him.

He rummaged around for another cigarette but couldn't find one. He felt like puking. He hadn't eaten all day and was dehydrated. He put his head into the kitchen sink and drank right from the tap. He paced back and forth. A frenzy of incoherent thoughts swirled inside him. He would submit to whatever overpowered him, masked his pain. Phoneless, he picked up the iPad, thinking he could find an old buddy to message on Facebook, maybe score a joint or two. When he pushed the home key a photo of him and Lucy came up. She'd made it the wallpaper, the two of them cuddling on the couch not long after the barbecue with her family. It felt so long ago, but it wasn't. How had so much happened? He didn't enter the passcode, just stared at the photo. They looked joyful, enamored with each other.

Could I actually be a father? What if I fuck it all up?

Jack heard Lucy tossing in the bed, emitting subtle sounds of discomfort. He wanted to care for her, to hold her. This thought made the others recede.

He loved Lucy. He would love their baby.

It could be that simple.

Summer Research

My parents were on vacation. They asked me to house-sit and to take care of their dog, a chocolate Labrador named Fudge they'd recently taken in from the reserve. That winter they'd moved from the reserve into what was once a nunnery in a small hamlet about five miles away. It was built in the 1950s as a lodging for nuns who operated the Indian residential school in a valley down the road. Out of principle, I had stayed away. My mother claimed to have known about the house, but it was a relative who'd been forced to attend the school who conveyed its history to me. I called my mother when I found out, and she simply said that she'd smudged the space to cleanse it and that all was well. I'd struggled with the ethical dilemma of whether to visit until this summer, when I had no choice but to drive up from the city to finish research for my doctoral thesis on public memory. I was interested in how the violence of the twentieth century lingered in people's lives today, both knowingly and unknowingly. I planned to interview locals as well as carry out a kind of experimental autoethnography—an examination of my emotional experience of the northern Albertan landscape. The house was bound up with this research.

The hamlet was located on a large lake that was once a glacial deposit and later a hub of Indigenous life and subsistence. In the last two decades, it had transformed from a sleepy enclave of locals to a bustling tourist destination. Several campsites and resorts now encroached upon the shoreline. My parents' house was a few yards away from the water, but it was directly across from an elementary school and thus mostly undesirable as a piece of real estate to the vacationers. Still, they paid exponentially more for it than they would have at the start of the century. Paying for property on one's own ancestral land was a paradox I still lost sleep over.

I PULLED INTO THE DRIVEWAY and at once the dog began howling. The house was situated in the middle of a small yard and beside it was a garage in front of which I parked. On the back door I found a housekeeping note that alerted me to the location of the spare key as well as instructions for Fudge's care. My parents were driving to the Rocky Mountains. They would be gone for a week, just enough time to visit towns in both Alberta and British Columbia. They hadn't ever really gone on vacation before, so I was happy to lend my time and attention. I let Fudge out and he peed gently on the deck—he was a submissive peer, demonstrating to me both his excitement and his passivity. He bared his teeth as a gesture of goodwill, and I gave him a few pats. He was medium-sized, stout, and had a stub of a tail; he had been run over as a pup, and his tail shattered. What was left wagged vigorously nonetheless.

Inside, I looked around hesitantly. I knew that the house had been renovated several times, but its bones remained the same since its initial construction—sometime in the fifties. The staircase in the middle of the house was narrow and steep; it led to two small bedrooms connected by a narrow tunnel in the wall, an architectural feature of some mid-twentieth-century homes, the purpose of which eluded me. I peeked inside and decided I hated the tunnel and would stay on the first floor to avoid it. I had no reason to be up there anyway. The bedroom I'd be sleeping in was a recent addition, next to the living area on the ground floor. The room felt modern and somewhat less haunted. But then again, I reminded myself, modernity was ridden with its own ghosts.

I lay on the bed and Fudge jumped up next to me, curling into a ball in the corner. I knew my parents didn't like Fudge to be on the furniture, but I let him stay. I reached into my bag and pulled out my copy of *Ghostly Matters*, a scholarly monograph by the cultural theorist Avery Gordon that was so central to my dissertation it had at this point accrued something akin to spiritual significance. In the introduction, Gordon noted that she was concerned with how various forms of domination affected "our shared conditions of living." "Conditions of living" had become an organizing concept in both my academic work and my life. All my thinking revolved around the question of how some conditions of living were more accurately conditions of premature death. Colonial capitalism was the structure in which the former transformed into the latter as a matter of policy and social relations. Gordon wrote, "haunting is . . . an animated state in which a repressed or unresolved social violence is making itself known, sometimes very directly, sometimes more obliquely." Symptoms of haunting, according to Gordon: when a home turned unfamiliar, when we felt disoriented in the middle of a regular day, when a blind spot suddenly reared into view and changed our way of thinking. It wasn't until grad school that my home region, all the small communities along the lake, piqued my philosophical interest. Reading Gordon, I realized that we all lived in the aftermath of unresolved social violence, yet we discussed it seldomly, if ever. I didn't believe that I could somehow magically alter what was thinkable, but I was invested in the concept all the same. To study the unthinkable was, in part, an effort to come to a deeper knowledge of my own selfhood.

In grad school, I asked my peers to describe their conditions of living. Most said precarious labor or racism or sexual exploration or a combination of all three. Everyone seemed so miserable, but most of us didn't desire any other way of life. To read and to think and sometimes to write was a way of life. Analysis was a practice we imbued with a deep and almost devotional seriousness. We desired with as much if not more intensity the shape of days that grad school made possible—an opportunity to exist outside conventional capitalist time. But, in the end, we were still subject to unconventional capitalist time all the same; our labor was exploited by other means. We were poorly paid, made into assistants for senior professors, enticed into believing in a job market that was more mythological than real. Despite what we did, despite how hard we worked, most of us would land near the bottom of the hierarchy of academic importance or outside it altogether.

In my current conditions of living I was trying to forget about that institutional noise. The only responsibilities I had were a duty to conduct research and to write, as well as to feed and walk the dog, to feed and keep myself busy. There was another thing: at my parents', my subjectivity loosened. I sometimes felt fragmented, less authentic. The environment didn't reflect my inner weather. To work at keeping myself together was a daily struggle.

I AWOKE TO FUDGE licking my face, his saliva warm and smelly. I got up, fetched his leash, and beckoned him to the door. He was jumping up and down, exuding glee. Had anyone ever said I "exuded glee"? It was a strange bit of description, and possibly a uniquely animal one. But I was an animal too, and so my happiness must also be animalistic.

It was muggy outside, and I immediately began to sweat. I patted my pockets to make sure I had my inhaler on me. Fudge pulled me in various directions. He wasn't accustomed to a leash and normally stayed within the confines of the yard, where there was plenty of grass for him to relieve himself on. I liked to walk, however, and wanted company and something at which to redirect the suspicion of strangers. A native man could incite symbolic alarm wherever he went, but especially so in rural Alberta. I hadn't been much of a presence in the small community in my adolescence and not at all as an adult. The community members would find me suspicious even if they were the ones who ultimately came from elsewhere.

I put on sunglasses and headphones and listened to a podcast about the personal essay. The interviewers argued that its rise was in part a result of an institutional favoring of experience at the expense of specialized knowledge. While I found most of the discussion riveting, I was bothered by the inattention to self-documentation as a political tool in the hands of marginalized people, as well as by a hierarchy of knowledge that my kokums and mosums would be placed at the bottom of. Surely, specialized knowledge emerged from normal life, I thought. My entire research project depended on it.

Fudge steered me toward a road that followed the lake's western shore, and I let him. Most of the houses I walked by had either been extensively renovated or newly built. One particularly large one jutted out into the water, supported by two beams jammed into rocks that held up a sprawling balcony. I imagined the water one day swallowing the house in an act of historical revenge. Eventually, Fudge and I reached an expanse of campsites that tourists frequented every summer. It occurred to me that I had never once visited any of the sites. No one in my family or social circle stayed there. The lots were mostly occupied by bulky fifth-wheel RVs, and from what I could see, all the campers were white. As I neared, one family stopped talking to watch me.

"Everything OK?" a middle-aged man in cargo shorts asked me.

"Uh, ya, totally," I said. "Just walking my dog."

"Do you need to do that right in front of my lot?"

I was caught off guard.

"And, while you're at it, maybe take off your sunglasses so I can see your face."

His dog started barking. Fudge lurched forward, but I pulled him back. The man put his arm out to signal to his dog to stay.

"I'll get going," I said.

He chuckled, and his wife muttered something that I assumed would fuel his anger. I began to walk away.

"Hey," he shouted. "Where are you staying around here? First time I'm seeing you."

I stopped. I could continue walking and simply avoid the area for the rest of my time here, though I'd planned to visit the abandoned residential school just yards away. Or I could stay

and defend myself on my peoples' territory. I valued the political importance of the latter enough to suppress my desire to
avoid conflict at all costs.

"I'm from here, actually," I said. "My family has lived on the
lake for centuries."

"Huh. Is that so."

I was so immersed in the world that I thought it would
destroy me. I thought of Judith Butler: language that is hurt-
ful exploits the way we are present, the ways we are available
to one another. That I immediately thought of philosophers in
a moment of distress was probably the opposite of a survival
instinct.

Fudge anxiously moved in and out of the space between
my legs.

Before the man could say more, his wife pulled him back by
the arm, though his eyes stayed fixed on me. When I was far
enough away, I hastened into a light jog. Fudge happily matched
my pace. Back inside my parents' house, I locked the door and
rested against it. Sweat poured down my forehead and into my
eyes. For a second, I couldn't see anything.

I texted my mom: "Just ran into a racist. Never leaving the
house again."

My phone: "Message failed to deliver."

THAT EVENING, I CHECKED MY EMAIL and saw I had a message from my supervisor reminding me of an upcoming dead-
line—I needed to submit a draft of a chapter. I had written very
little of it. Maybe I could use the confrontation with the racist as an anecdote in my thesis, I thought. The desire to trans-
form a traumatic experience into research mere hours after it

occurred was probably a trauma response. There was no way to differentiate my research from what happened in any given day in my life. I was indistinguishable from my research. And so I responded to my supervisor with a long-winded account of the trip so far. I ended the email with a postscript that he didn't have to reply if what I wrote seemed too personal. I was always forgetting that the personal was supposed to be subsumed within the intellectual, subjugated by it. I wanted desperately to be an intellectual, but all my curiosities were personal.

I OPTED NOT TO TAKE FUDGE on an evening walk. I sat on the balcony and watched him roam around the yard instead. He pooped behind a massive spruce tree. I didn't pick it up because I hated the idea of wearing a tiny plastic bag like a glove in order to do so. Waves of pollen cascaded onto me with every gust of wind. I sneezed, then sneezed again, so I called Fudge and went back in.

In bed I scrolled through Twitter. It was Pride month, so there were several jokes about the gay condition. One user wrote: "when is gay invincibility month?" I liked the tweet. The idea of orienting social life around our invincibility and not our pride was more appealing to me; it seemed less likely to be disfigured by corporate interests. It also gestured to a continuing practice of defiance and resistance that I considered my work a part of. I wasn't dating anyone, nor was I seeking to hook up while housesitting. I would still enact my sexual politics if only because to be queer in rural Alberta was to be a one-person protest against the normative. This hypervisibility, obviously, also made me into a moving target.

I debated leaving a reading lamp on while I slept. I wasn't exactly scared, but now that the day had receded, I couldn't help thinking about the nuns. It was sociologically likely that they had done considerable harm while living in the house. The school had operated for decades. Indigenous children from all over the province had been forcibly detained there. Where did the nuns come from? What did they do when at the house? Did they think about their actions, about the violence they were implicated in? How much did the language of Catholicism shroud that violence? I had gone to Catholic school, so I understood that God wasn't an entity but rather a set of ideas that could be put to terrible use. Only certain people instantiated "God's image"; the effort to sculpt others in that image was itself a horror story. In the end, I fell asleep with the lamp on.

I WOKE UP standing in the bathroom, uncertain what time it was. The light bled and whirled. I didn't remember getting out of bed. My pulse was racing dangerously. I had a strong urge to check behind the shower curtain, which was something I did often as a child. When I peeled the plastic lining back, there was a woman dressed in a long black gown standing in the tub, dripping with water. I couldn't see her face. I began to scream, then fell to the ground trying to get away, hitting my head against the toilet.

I woke up in bed in a sweat, my breathing ragged. When I got up to find my inhaler, Fudge let out a small whine. I felt calmed by his presence. I switched on several lights in the house and took two puffs from my inhaler; my lungs welcomed the medication, and almost instantly my normal rhythm was restored. Back in bed, I called Fudge over and he nestled into my left side, letting out a gentle sigh. His small animal body made me feel less lonely and then, moments later, lonelier than ever.

I TEXTED MY MOM first thing in the morning.

Me: Had a dream I saw a woman in your bathtub.

Mom: You should meet with my medium! Maybe someone is trying to contact you from the other side.

Me: Even if I believed that stuff, why would I want to talk to a colonial nun?

Mom: Colonial nun! LOL

Mom: I just told your dad what you said and we can't stop laughing.

Me: I'm serious!

Mom: Trust me, the medium is AMAZING!

My mom had called me after every session she had with the medium. For some reason, the medium was always bringing up my love life—or lack thereof. She envisioned me getting married, having a large wedding. It seemed that her visions of gay life were constrained by the rural milieu; to be gay was to slide into heterosexual scripts. If anything, I wanted to explode the heterosexual scripts of my upbringing. As a joke, I debated confronting the medium about her homonormativity.

Me: Fine, but I'm not paying for it!

AT NOON I WALKED FUDGE into a nearby patch of boreal forest. I was worried about ticks and had been obsessively googling their incidence in northern Alberta, so I'd slathered myself in bug repellent before leaving the house. Because this made me feel slimy and non-human, the walk was brief. After, I drove to the reserve located on the other side of the train tracks, which functioned as a de facto border, an ever-present reminder of the ongoing maintenance of the colonial state.

I arrived at the Band Office ahead of a scheduled interview with the Chief, a distant relative of mine. He'd been in office for several terms, overseeing an economic boom of sorts. Many reserves continued to be so underfunded that even minor budgetary increases could alter everyday life. On ours, more houses were built, and a new gas station and community center were under construction. I wanted to discuss with him this boom as well as the nation's effort to identify unmarked graves at the property where the residential school had been.

Once inside, his administrative assistant called me into a room.

Three large printers hummed beside me.

"I'm so sorry," she said, "but the Chief has been called into an emergency meeting. He won't be able to talk today after all."

I hadn't considered the possibility that the interview wouldn't happen. It was one of the few that my thesis seemed to require.

"Is everything all right?" I asked, accepting that my intellectual desires didn't govern the Chief's life.

"It's about the graves—that's all I can say." Her face registered a sorrow at once profound and deeply private.

"I understand," I said, taking on some of her sorrow. "Can he meet in the coming days?"

"Uh, yes, how about on Monday, noon?"

"That's perfect, thank you."

"It's nice to see you around," she added. "Your mom and I were friends back in the day."

I hugged her, even though I couldn't remember her name.

IN THE CAR, I entertained invasive thoughts that my research trip would be futile, and that my dissertation wouldn't amount to much and therefore I would have to leave academia. My supervisor was a social scientist, and I was more instinctively a humanist; truthfully, the interviews were a way of appeasing his academic sensibilities. I mostly wanted to write about my own subjective experience, to analyze my family's self-mythologies. A pang of resentment arose, but I suppressed it. I reminded myself that the trip wasn't yet over and I had interviews lined up for next week.

My phone pinged with a message from my mom.

Mom: I talked to the medium, she has an opening tomorrow!

My cynicism had softened. Maybe I could approach a meeting with a medium as an important scholarly undertaking. Mediums claimed to speak on behalf of a collective, a whole community of living and dead. That this medium was a wealthy white woman wasn't politically irrelevant. Being alive in this century meant always reminding people that everything was somehow politically relevant. In talking with the medium, I could attempt to examine how some people and not others were authorized to speak on behalf of an entire community.

Me: OK, send me the address.

With the afternoon suddenly free, I decided to drive around the reserve. I took iPhone photos out of the driver's side window of some anti-authority graffiti, stop signs bearing both English and Cree, our ancestral language. Maybe the photos could count as a primary source. Social scientists were always having to think of everything as potential data. I was potential data. So were my memories. My future self was a result of the social reproduction of that data. Maybe I was a social scientist after all—if not because of my supervisor's influence then because I was always calculating my livability with old and new information about the past and the present. An Indigenous person had to be a sociologist of his own life. It was nothing if not tiring.

THE MEDIUM'S OFFICE was in a building owned by a resource extraction company in a nearby industry town. The drive was short. I listened to "Break My Soul" by Beyoncé on repeat. Would quitting my job, as Beyoncé instructed, really save my soul if what my job boiled down to was "thinking"? I wondered this until I turned the engine off.

The sign on the medium's door read "Angelic Answers," the name she'd given her business. Mom noted I shouldn't mention anything financial. The medium didn't want people thinking what she did was purely transactional even though she charged two hundred dollars a session. I was surprised to find that the room in which she held the meetings was minimally furnished. The medium sat behind a large oak desk in the middle of the room, flanked on either side by a house plant and a multiheaded lamp. She was middle-aged and wore an expression of diplomatic interest, as though interest were something we were inherently owed as people in the world. It felt vacuous, like a formality.

"Have a seat," she said, perhaps noticing I was tense. "I'm Helen. Your mother said we had something urgent to discuss."

"Something like that," I said.

"Well, let's get started. Do you have a personal object I can hold?"

"A what? I didn't know. Oh, uh, I'm guessing my phone won't do?"

Helen looked at me intently. "No, something more sentimental, something that tells me a bit about your values and connects me to your spirit."

Had anyone ever connected to my spirit? I patted my pockets, hoping something would magically appear, then I remembered I had a photo of my parents in their twenties in my wallet. I retrieved it, passing it to Helen. She barely looked at it, closing it instead between her palms.

"Now," she said, "we need a way to open up a door between our world and theirs—that is, those who have passed on."

I nodded tentatively, though it seemed foolish to create that kind of portal.

"Usually, brief contact is all I need." She put the photo on the table and opened her hand to me. I grabbed it. She closed her eyes.

"I want you to visualize someone you've lost."

"What if I haven't lost anyone?" I asked.

At this she opened one of her eyes. "What brings you here again? Your mom didn't specify."

"Well," I said hesitantly, "I had a dream the other night of a woman dressed in black in her house."

She nodded as though she had expected me to say this. I felt I had given her too much information.

"Ah, yes. Can you describe the woman?"

"Honestly, that's the best I can do. I didn't see her face."

"When spirits don't show their faces to us it can mean several things. Malevolence and fear, for example. Or it can mean there isn't a strong enough connection to the host—i.e., you."

"I don't think I want there to be a strong connection."

"So, it's not a conversation or message you're after?"

"No, not really. If anything, maybe a bit more clarity." I realized then that I probably needed to see a psychoanalyst and not a medium, someone who could assist with the work of dream interpretation. It wasn't the dead I needed to connect with, but my own subconscious, itself a realm of the deceased. Perhaps all psychoanalysts were also mediums.

Helen closed her eyes again. "I see a big woman in braids, long, sprawling braids. There's a tipi too, it appears to have been painted on . . . Do these evoke anything for you?"

I pondered, then grew annoyed. All tropes, easy Indigenous imagery. "I don't think so."

"Could the woman be a great grandmother or even further back than that?"

"None of them were large as far as I know," I said, "nor have I seen photos of anyone in braids."

She let go of my hand. "The woman might represent an opposing energy, the opposite of the woman dressed in black. Maybe she represents cultural continuity. Maybe she wants to protect you."

"I suppose my ancestors would want to defend me," I said.

"I think we have to ask the menacing woman to leave, to tell her she isn't needed or wanted," Helen said.

"How do we do that?"

"You just have to say it out loud."

That's all? "All right. I banish thee," I said. Thee?

Helen smiled. "Repeat after me: I do not wish to connect with you. I have nothing for you. My ancestors are here, and we rebuke you."

I repeated the three sentences even though it embarrassed me. I waited for the atmosphere of the room to shift or for something inside me to change. Nothing happened.

"You seem to be carrying a lot of grief, by the way," she said.

I thought about this. What were the conditions of my grief? There were all the dissatisfactions of graduate school, but I'd hardly classify them as worthy of grief. Ultimately, I knew, my sadness was correlated with the trauma of colonialism.

"Yes," she added, grimacing. "Your spirit is so heavy."

FUDGE WAS WAITING FOR ME when I returned. As soon as I opened the door, he bolted across the highway and into the grassy field behind the school. I chased after him, only to find him eating bear poop near a trash can. I tugged him away, fastening him to the leash. When I looked up, I saw the man from the campsite watching us. His children were using the playground. I felt surveilled, uneasy. I walked back to the house but turned around one last time. He was still watching me even as he disappeared into the horizon, but I swear I saw him make a gun with his hand and point it at me.

THAT NIGHT I WATCHED TV absent-mindedly. I contemplated whether Helen had rid me of the nun's ghostly presence. I decided it was unlikely, but how I felt about Helen's work was evolving. It was her job to bear the community's grief, I just wasn't willing to give mine to her. She performed a form of emotional labor and was compensated for it. She wasn't a medium, that much was clear, and perhaps that constituted fraud, but still she made space for people to discuss their pain. In rural Alberta, that was urgent and necessary work.

I fell asleep on the couch and woke to Fudge barking at the staircase. I moved to the bedroom and called him to me. We fell asleep cuddling.

———

THE NEXT MORNING, I remembered that the priest at the church down the road saw people for confession on Saturdays. I opted not to ask my mom if this was still the case. I didn't want her to think I suddenly needed religious salvation. Plus I had questions about the house and the residential school that I didn't want to burden her with. I was familiar with the church anyways; I'd attended mass on occasion with family throughout the years.

Would a priest tell the truth about the colonial past? I had to find out. I got dressed and walked over. I pushed open the heavy oak doors and stepped inside. It smelled of dust and old furniture. The priest oversaw a modest parish, serving just a couple dozen churchgoers in the region. I sat in a pew at the back. The priest walked in as I thumbed through a worn, gilt-edged Bible.

"Are you here for confession?" His voice was so soft it barely reached me.

"Yes, as long as that's not an inconvenience."

"None whatsoever. Please," he said, motioning toward the confessional.

As soon as I stepped into the narrow compartment of the confession booth, I felt confined. A small placard outlined the process. I recited a short prayer, the father engaging as I did. When we finished, he asked if I had sinned and if I would like to atone for those sins, betraying that the answer to the former was always yes.

"Actually, Father, I want to ask your opinion about a dream I had." This was only partly true.

"Oh, well, yes, of course, child."

"My parents moved into the white house just up the road, the one that used to be a nunnery. I'm sure you're aware. I dreamed of a nun standing in the bathtub. Frankly, it was terri-fying." I thought about how to formulate the question. I knew it would sound rigid, awkward, but I asked it anyways. "What do you make of that?"

It was so dark in the box that I struggled to visualize him. I wasn't certain he'd even heard me.

"I'm sorry," he said, "I'm afraid I don't make much of it. Maybe," he conceded, "it represents a loss of faith. Have you lost faith?"

"I'm not a Catholic," I admitted.

"I'd be happy to talk in my office if you'd like to discuss what we do here."

"Well, I am baptized and confirmed. But that's beside the point. I'm wondering if you know anything about the nuns who lived at the nunnery."

He fell silent. I cleared my throat.

"Maybe I can rephrase," I said, emboldened. "What do you make of the legacy of residential schools?"

"That isn't really a topic of conversation for confession. You're meant to confess your sins."

"I'm not asking you to bear any responsibility, Father. But you must agree that what happened in those schools was sin-ful." I felt uncomfortable using the language of confession, but I wanted the conversation, however strained, to continue.

"Well, the official stance of the Church—"

I interrupted. "What's your stance?"

"I don't see how what I think matters."

I thought this over. I suppose he was right.

"Do you think those nuns atoned?"

I heard him stand up. "Let's step outside," he said.

Daylight burst into the box when I opened the door, a meta-phor, perhaps, for how I had broken the form of the confession. I hadn't participated in the mode of self-subjugation it required.

I wasn't an object of pity that needed to be relinquished from the past. I felt satisfied by this.

"Again, I'm sorry that I can't be more helpful," he said, gesturing to the door.

"Thank you for your time, Father," I said. I wasn't sure if I meant it.

I left the church and returned to my regular life.

A TEXT. MOM: "We're going deeper into the mountains today. Likely won't have service until Monday. Love y'all!"

IN THE EVENING I felt sick. I assumed I had a case of heat exhaustion. The sun had pummeled us all weekend. It was the first heat wave of the summer, and I lay on the couch while Fudge hid in the shade under the back porch. I almost forgot to let him back in before bed.

That night I slept terribly, waking up several times, once to urinate, then twice more for no apparent reason. Finally, around two in the morning, I fell solidly asleep. At four I woke to a torrent of noise coming from upstairs. Had I left the door unlocked? Was the house being burgled? I tried to call my mom, then remembered her message. I understood that calling the police would put me in added danger, so I didn't do that. I went to the kitchen to grab a frying pan instead. The noises grew louder. Furniture was being knocked around. I approached the staircase, my fear vibrating around me.

I opened Fudge's dog gate and made my way up the steep, narrow staircase to the second floor, turning on as many lights as possible. The door to the first room was slightly ajar. I peered inside—nothing. The door to the second room was wide open. I hadn't remembered opening it. I felt less like a person and more like an animal. I passed through the threshold, the frying pan hoisted into the air, when Fudge came bounding toward me.

"Fudge, what are you doing up here?" I said, more incredulous than angry. "I'm so damn happy to see you!"

My body settled. I looked around the room. Fudge had knocked over two lamps, a small bookcase, an old TV. I picked everything up, making sure nothing was broken. When I plugged the TV in, the sudden static scared me, but I laughed it off. I told Fudge to go to bed and heard his paws make their way down the narrow steps. Good boy, I thought.

I was still kneeling on the ground when the hallway light flickered on and off, then went out entirely.

"What the fuck?" I muttered.

My chest started heaving, my airways constricting. I couldn't remember where I put my inhaler. I felt trapped inside my body, glued to the floor. Then the light in the room I was in went out too. My eyes struggled to adjust to the darkness. I looked into the tunnel, and something compelled me to crawl through it. I saw a faint glow of light from the other room, a beacon of sorts. I exhaled, drawing out long breaths, then army-crawled through the darkness. I thought I felt a presence behind me, so I barreled forward. In the adjoining room, the silence was at first eerie, then comforting. I looked around; everything seemed to be in its rightful place. I no longer detected anything behind me. I felt my heart slowing, my body relieving some of its tension. I let out a sharp sigh, then I composed myself as best I could.

I stepped into the hallway and in it stood a figure at the top of the staircase. It was the woman from my dream. For the first time, I could see her face.

My Diary

At last, I have finished unpacking. The drive from Toronto
was long and exhausting. The prairies were expansive,
which made the sky loom oppressively over me. For a few
hours, I went without cell service. I listened to biblical
radio to fill the silence. An evangelical argued that all the
death surrounding us was our chance to appreciate "the
sanctity of life." It seemed to me a bleak worldview, that we
should pretend to be holier despite the counterevidence.
I thought about the concept of the holy—if it could be
stripped of religious connotations—instead of paying
closer attention to the roads. I'm lucky enough to have
had kinds of sex that felt sacred, after which living felt
more possible. But that's not what the Catholics meant.
I suppose I'm thinking about all of this because I've just
moved back to my ancestral territory, the place of my
childhood, where the traces of a nineteenth-century Catholic
missionary presence are endlessly evident. To exist in
northern Alberta, I have to defend against all the traumas
the pursuit of a holy life was (and is still) connected with.

I've been in what many aspiringly call "midlife" for a while now; I always thought I'd be dead by this age. So this diary is something of a record of an expired life. No, maybe *exceeded* is a better word. I have exceeded the limits of my inherited life-chances. My late twenties felt like midlife. Even so, several of my friends had already died by then. The world doesn't terrify me anymore. I've already rehearsed plenty of its calamitous scenes. I just left the city I'd lived in for over two decades because I want to spend the last part of my life in my homeland. Whenever I write *homeland* I see the ghostly possibility of the nonword HOMOLAND. I wish my homeland was queerer. That would have solved the problems I had growing up—there was so much to contend with and no schema to reduce the scale of contention to something manageable. I'm back now to imbue the landscape with whatever queer currents I can muster. Is it possible to be a singular person and alter the current of a whole landscape, make it queerer? Maybe that's how I should think of the next phase of my life and art practice, as an attempt to alter the current of northern Alberta's emotional biome. Maybe it's silly or grandiose to think of the relocation as an extension of my art practice. Maybe it's the only way I'll keep surviving.

I'm content with the art I've made and exhibited throughout my career. But mostly what I find myself thinking about are the moments I experienced so much love I couldn't bear it. I keep thinking about nostalgia, about how it requires us to pity our present time, which is all we really have. But I also have a use for nostalgia. It reminds me that at times I was alive and it didn't hurt, that I haven't always been stuck underneath the surface of living, as I have felt with the regularity of new seasons. Despite that, sometimes I stood triumphantly on the earth and didn't shudder.

I woke up a little after 2 am terribly alert. The house felt
unfamiliar, foreign, and so my body felt foreign in it. I sat
at the kitchen table, which belonged to the previous owner.
It's a large oak, the kind I always imagined having but the
apartments I lived in in Toronto were all so small. I purchased
the plot of land and the house as soon as I saw it on the
Realtor's website. The property is surrounded by the boreal
forest. The photographs looked like a painting. I wanted to
situate myself in a painting, though I've never been a painter
myself. The property is a few miles from the reserve I come
from. The lake is a short walk away. I'm both pained and
exhilarated by the new beginning. I'm unobligated. There's
nothing I have to do in the near future, no one expects
anything from me. The future is something I can breathe in.
I can breathe in time like words, like complete sentences.

I woke midmorning, later than I intended. The world-
historical heat pervaded the house. I opened some windows,
but the mosquitoes and flies invaded. I feared that the rest
of the decade, which had just begun, would be full of world-
historical weather events. Coffee soothed me for a short time.
I'd almost given up my coffee machine, thinking I'd revert to
a more manual set of daily practices, but I'm glad that notion
didn't hold. I didn't have to pretend to be in another era.

I'm seated on the porch in my underwear, light blue briefs I've
owned for a decade. The fabric is tattered, and in a certain
light you can see the outline of my genitals. The sun today is
exacting. It exposes something in me—that my inner weather
is erratic. I feel anxious, not serene. I banked on serenity
and peace awaiting me. But perhaps that was foolish, as
I've returned here innumerable times as an adult and often
experienced a strong desire to leave after just a few days. It
always felt as though I had to put my true being on pause.
What was a true being, really, though? A few good years, a
handful of evocative ideas. I figure I can make do in this state
of suspended reality, as long as this diary keeps me tethered
to the present. Text has always been a part of my art practice.
In my thirties, I exhibited a series of textual wallpapers
composed of statements like "A LIFE: IT RUNS OUT"
and "GRIEF IS A FORM OF INTERNAL SILENCE."
They toured the continent. I also covered my studio in
them. For years, the sentences sheltered me, kept me rooted
in my body. It felt like I'd finally made visible an aspect of
my thinking that the purely visual eclipsed or suppressed.

I find myself imagining other people will read this diary. Some art history grad student will find it in my archive decades after I've died. This would be both lucky and unlucky. The thought makes the practice feel a bit shameful. Or, maybe, the shame represents the audience of my future selves? How many more selves can I still bring into being? The mere thought of doing so tires me.

Perhaps I'm inventing my own archive. This diary will serve as the ur-text that puts my previous artworks into context. The context is that I'm suffering and the world is dazzlingly incoherent. To return to the site of one's upbringing shouldn't be an experience of incoherence. Somehow, it is.

It's almost midnight and still there are traces of sunlight in the sky. It wasn't until I was an adult that I learned that where I was from was in the subarctic. The knowledge clarified something for me, that I was a product of a geologically specific region. Who I could be or become was circumscribed. Part of me would always be someone whom the cold drove inward. This sense of inwardness has felt apparent since arriving at the house. The voice in my head feels pervasive, always rippling, like water.

This morning Aunt Lorna stopped by for coffee. I was still in bed when she knocked at the door. I hadn't told anyone that I'd moved back, but a distant cousin had seen me from afar on a walk yesterday and word spread. She'd heard someone bought the property and assumed correctly that it was me. Lorna was my mother's younger sister; she kept in touch after my parents passed away. I wished I had moved back when they were still alive, but even just five years ago I was fixed on being in the city, out east, surrounded by strangers, by art. I wanted a house and a few acres so that my grief could have space to expand. If grief is compressed, if it has nowhere to go, it mutates. It was mutating inside me in Toronto. I didn't know what to do with it rattling around inside me like I was pure negative space. I wanted to come back to deposit it in the world, put it down somewhere else, somewhere familiar.

Lorna caught me up on the local goings-on: petty dramas, political thrillers. Most of it sounded like a novel about characters I only vaguely understood. She invited me to a family dinner on the reserve that weekend. I told her I'd try to make it.

After she left I walked through the forest. As a kid I'd watched families of deer graze all the time. Some days I was afraid of their silence, their unknowable interiorities. Now I found what I didn't know about them the most meaningful. I saw traces of their presence here and there: tufts of fur embedded in tree bark, sets of tracks in the soft grass. I puzzled over what kinds of art I could make in collaboration with the forest and the animals. My practice had been so theoretical, far from land-based. I was interested in ideas and language and new media. Most of my work was digital or made from textiles. In the forest, where it was mercifully cooler, I imagined reinventing my aesthetic, making art for non-humans, art that was meant to decompose, art I would immediately have to surrender.

I fetched groceries in a nearby town. Most of my memories attached to the place were incomplete or uninteresting. It had changed very little—same high school, some new stores, a new hospital. I moved quickly through the grocery store, avoiding the glances of other shoppers. As I was paying, I noticed in my peripheral vision a man I went to high school with, T. He was the first person I'd had sex with. We were both so ravenous and inexperienced—it happened, then we never talked about it. Last I heard, in my early twenties, he was in a serious relationship with a woman. I hadn't thought about him much since. There were other men, ones I was able to have conversations with about our desires. Eventually T took up less and less space in my mind, until the image of him whittled down to a brief memory of the despair of youth. Here he was in embodied space with me again. I was surprised that he was still handsome. He retained the carefree energy I'd been drawn to as a teen. Like me, he had a dad bod. Our eyes locked, then I turned away to pull out my credit card. On the drive back, I thought about our short friendship. It was one of convenience, of proximity, and perhaps so was our one hookup. I thought about my last relationship, from about two years ago. It, too, was brief. The man found me "overly ruminative" and complained that he never knew what I was thinking. Because I was open to something fleeting or something long-term without overt preference, I didn't push too hard against his resistance. We stopped talking because of that. I hadn't had sex since. The apps weighed me down these days, made me feel like an object and not a person. I figured I'd settle into rural life with little sexual expectation. Northern Alberta seemed to me to afford the opposite of sexual vitality. Even so, I masturbated as soon as I returned to the house, aroused still by the erotic image of T. I'm writing this with semen on my chest.

It was so hot I had a cold bath, then sat in the shade behind the house, naked. I don't remember it ever getting this hot up here in my lifetime. On my phone, I read a few news articles about the "heat dome"—an apt name, a metaphor that feels real at the level of physiology. When a metaphor becomes real it isn't a failure of language; it's a symptom of historical change.

I rose early because of the humidity. I felt irritated, headache-y.
I opted not to have coffee and walked to the water instead.
The lake was large, though not enormous. The path to the
shore was unkept, the grass dying, yellowing—everything
evoked death. I walked into the water until I was knee-
deep. I could see minnows swirling around underneath. In
the distance I spotted a boat, likely a fisherman wanting to
get a couple hours in before the midday heat. Afterwards
I decided to walk the two miles to the cemetery where my
parents are buried. It was the first time I'd visited since the
funeral. Someone had kept their graves tidy. I was grateful
for that but vowed to do so myself for the foreseeable future.
I recognized the last names on most of the headstones,
though I couldn't quite envision the people themselves. My
parents had never left northern Alberta, except for a brief
stint in a lumbering town to the east. I understood that
throughout my entire adulthood they missed me immensely;
I was their only child. I didn't know how to slow the pace of
my life to spend more time with them. I often encouraged
them to visit me in Toronto, to make the drive out, but
they always said they were too old for the excursion and
avoided air travel. I hadn't done enough to sideline my own
desires. I knelt at their graves and became sunburnt.

I received an email from T. He must've found my email address online; I think it's still listed on the website of the art college I taught at when they needed an adjunct. "Is it true?" he wrote. "Are you in town? Were you at the grocery store yesterday? Let's grab a beer or something." I was somehow nervous, after all these years. "Why don't you stop by my new place?" I wrote back. "I'm free tonight." He replied almost immediately. "Send the address. I'll arrive around 8."

I called Lorna to tell her I wouldn't be able to make it to dinner, that something came up. "Just stop by whenever," she said, which I knew she meant. "We've missed you." I tidied the house, put things in their rightful places. It was still midafternoon, but I felt overwhelmed with anticipation. I googled T but nothing came up. For all I knew he was firmly heterosexual. Maybe he really did just want to reconnect as friends. I planned to douche and to trim my pubes anyways.

I sat in the shade outside and admired the trees, aspens and spruce, both shaking with life despite the heat. I read the other night that the boreal forest was already registering the detrimental effects of climate change— some scientists predict the boreal will recede north and die off in some southern stretches, where I live, which seems impossible but not unimaginable given the twenty-first century's catastrophic state of affairs. It would be an affront to the region's ancestral memory. The boreal forest is a repository of both beauty and grief. I have to bear the forest's grief and not simply expect it to bear mine.

Restless, I thumbed through my copy of Woolf's *To the Lighthouse*, one of my favorite books about being an artist. A long time ago, I had underlined the following: "Who knows what we are, what we feel? Who knows even at the moment of intimacy, This is knowledge?"

I've lived at an emotional distance from myself for the last five years. My self-knowledge is imprecise. Why did I leave Toronto so abruptly? I have yet to formally tell anyone—my friends think I'm still in my old condo. What do I want from all of this? I had to leave the city to grieve properly. I want to live differently. I want the freedom of a modest existence. I want my living to amount to a kind of artfulness. Is that too much to want? It shouldn't be; it shouldn't be.

T is asleep in my bed. I'm writing this as quietly as possible
at the kitchen table. He arrived a little before 8:00 with a
case of beer. I typically avoided alcohol, but I indulged him.
At first, he was distant and seemingly shelled up in the kind
of rural masculinity men around here wore with ease, but
I or the alcohol eventually coaxed him out of that strange
performance (who was his audience?). We sat in my living
room, and he told me about his life. After high school, he
got a job at the local mill. He worked there for two decades.
He dated women but never settled down. He hadn't had
kids, had been careful not to. He thought that one day he
might move to the city to reinvent himself. That was easier
said than done, he told me. He works nowadays as a laborer,
contract work that keeps him afloat. His life's story was
really that straightforward, that succinct. He narrated it as
though it were an elegy, as though he had already died.

I told him a little about me: my career, the men I dated, the
happiness they brought me. T seemed to wince at the latter
and withdraw slightly. "I've thought about our time together
a lot over the years," he said eventually. I didn't know what to
say, but I knew our longing was the truth about us. "Seeing
you the other day felt like a fucking miracle," he said while
looking out the window. We ached for each other the rest
of the evening. I brushed against him; he kept placing his
hand on my back. At 11:00, I asked if I could kiss him. He
said yes. Kissing him made me feel young again, it collapsed
time. We moved to my bed, where we kissed more deeply.
He fucked me more tenderly than I've ever been fucked.
He looked me in the eyes, and I saw that he was tearful. I
understood that he wasn't thinking about anything else. I
want to fuck him too, when he's ready and courageous enough

(the prospect of being his first penetrative lover is thrilling, admittedly). I've been with enough men to know when the connection is real and when it isn't, when it is shared, when it is electrifying and earthy. I want him to be around, in my vicinity. I want to figure out if he's someone I could fall in love with. Yes, we've only just reconnected, but so much feels possible again. Unlike Woolf's painter at the end of *To the Lighthouse*, this moment of intimacy is humming in my mind with absolute certainty; it has made me clearer to myself.

Outside, the stars are gleaming. They're so bright the living room is illuminated; I can see the shape of everything around me. The forest, conversely, is dense with night. At this hour, it must be silently bustling with life, with animals attempting to live a little longer. In bed with T I felt dense with the desire to live longer. If nothing else, I know that it's rare to feel as desperate to see what the future holds as I do right now, as I did after the first time he and I had sex. I didn't realize I still had that degree of desperation in me. It's a relief.

I can still smell him on me.

Various People

AT DAWN PAUL LOOKS AT HIS HOUSE from inside the midsized SUV he bought with future children in mind. It's the future, and there are no children. Paul and his wife, Julia, live busy lives. He's the director of a nonprofit, and she's a head nurse at a downtown hospital. Over the aughts and into the present decade, their careers blossomed. They earned promotions and raises, accrued more power than Indigenous peoples typically did in large institutions and organizations, and so they ascended into the upper middle class, although Paul would never consider himself a member of its ranks, coming as he does from a working-class family. Julia, however, comes from wealth. Her grandfather served as the chief of their reserve for two decades in the twentieth century, overseeing a period of prosperity while other bands in the region remained underfunded. Her grandfather embraced resource extraction, establishing a reserve-owned and -operated company that continues to employ over a hundred people. Julia's parents lived in the city; she never lived on their reserve. Julia doesn't like to talk about any of this. It's no longer something to be proud of. To be rich and native is no longer an anomaly, but, in some circles, to be a native capitalist, as her grandfather was, is a cause for contempt.

Paul and Julia are in their late forties; twenty years have passed since they first moved in together. They live in a detached home in a neighborhood that effectively connects the suburb to the city. Their neighbors are all bourgeois and non-native. Sometimes Paul feels uneasy walking alone. People glance nervously at him or even cross the street as he approaches. One time a woman yelled at him to keep back, claiming she had a weapon. Paul tries to laugh off these encounters, otherwise he'd go mad. Sometimes he questions why they moved into the neighborhood to begin with. They were both fixed on the idea, entranced by what the neighborhood symbolized. It seemed to radiate a purity, both moral and social. Paul didn't realize until later that his being there threatened that symbolic order. He would never be unconditionally welcomed into it and so eventually learned to derive solace from this exclusion. He wouldn't be assimilated.

Their house is big but uninteresting. It's like all the other houses on the block, save for small differences. Theirs has an attic, which makes it the tallest. They have so much extra space in their lives that they don't know what to do with it all.

For a few minutes, Paul watches the shadow of Julia moving around upstairs. She'll be off to work in an hour or so. He's about to drive northward, to his reserve, where his mother, Louise, is dying.

THE DRIVE IS LONG, seemingly unending. Paul is speeding. The highway winds through the boreal forest, passing expanses of farmers' fields that have already been harvested.

The vibrancy of the autumn leaves—orange, red, yellow—feels ironic to Paul; soon they'll be dead plant matter on the forest floor. As he hurtles north, a subtle panic pervades him—everything around him is in some state of disintegration.

About an hour from the reserve, Paul pulls over to urinate beside an aspen tree. The aspen is young, as are most of the trees along this stretch of highway, which a forest fire decimated not long ago. He once read that aspens have an extensive root system that allows them to bounce back after natural disasters and logging. So much survives, Paul thinks, even through massive destruction. It's as though the trees can't help but survive. In people, this is a virtuous quality. Paul, however, has seldom felt virtuous.

Back in the SUV, Paul thinks about the distance between who he is and who he could've been. The looming presence of death makes the distance brighter. In his twenties, he wanted to live a normal life: to own a house, to have a stable job, to get married. He has done all these things, and so for a time his happiness was indubitable. He wanted these things because so many natives were denied them. He didn't want to be a native who was denied anything. This was an impossible desire: there was no way Paul could exist outside history. Now Paul is more alert to this conundrum; he doesn't try to sublimate or repress it.

His marriage has been uneventful, and for this he is grateful. But what has his small life made possible and what has it curtailed? Can he start over in his forties, remake himself? What would Julia think? He contemplates how inseparable she is from her economic status, how she has never expressed a longing for a different way of living. For the rest of the drive, Paul is left with the idea that if he doesn't change his life, he'll have made a terrible mistake.

A NUMBER OF PEOPLE on the reserve have died of cancer recently, and Paul, nearing the reserve, wonders whether this pattern is more than coincidental. The years of boiled water advisories, pollution from industry—it seems correlative. He wonders if anyone is studying this and makes a note in his phone to email a researcher he knows at the university. His own work, in Indigenous advocacy, has consumed and exhausted him, so he has taken a month-long leave. He couldn't hold space for his grief and his work at the same time. He may spend the entire time on the reserve. He hinted to Julia that she should come with him, but she either didn't notice or chose not to pick up on the hints. He couldn't outright ask her. He was too afraid she'd say no.

LOUISE'S HOUSE LOOKS EXACTLY AS IT DID when Paul was a child. It's a rancher that sits behind a large field used for making hay bales (Paul's cousin is a cattle farmer). As a kid, Paul would climb onto the bales and pretend he was a giant. Louise would watch him from the porch, smiling. He fell backwards off one once and Louise had to run into the field to retrieve him. He had to be treated for a concussion, and so was forbidden from playing on them ever again. The field is empty today, save for one bale, and Paul is unexpectedly heavy-hearted. Soon, it will be just him.

A son without a mother and a father is a bit of forgotten history, a lost country of the mind.

Paul pulls into the driveway and turns the engine off. He continues looking at the lone hay bale, it must've been deliberately left behind during the harvest. He winces.

INSIDE, VARIOUS PEOPLE stand around Louise, who is sitting upright in a bed that has been installed in the living room. Photographs still clutter the walls. He tiptoes behind the small crowd, not wanting to disrupt the flow of conversation. It takes him a minute to notice that a few of them are speaking in Cree. Paul is struck by how seamlessly Louise converses in her ancestral tongue, which he hasn't heard her do in a while. He remembers moments from his childhood when Louise would run into an acquaintance and they'd speak Cree. Paul would ask her to translate, but sometimes Louise wouldn't be able to. "I couldn't quite understand because he mumbled at the end," she'd say. Years later, while at the university, Paul reflected more deeply on this; he thought it was amazing that in order for a Cree sentence to make sense it had to be spoken as carefully as possible. What would the world look like if we all had to treat language with that much care? All he speaks is English, which is both blunt and ugly.

A woman Paul doesn't recognize leans toward him: "She wanted to talk to someone in Cree. She's been asking all day."

"What are they talking about?"

"I'm not fluent," she says, "but I think they're talking about the dead."

WHEN THE VISITORS LEAVE, Paul can at last get a clear look at Louise. Her face is gaunt. She's wearing a head scarf and a long cotton dress. He can't remember the last time he saw her in a dress, if ever. She has always been small, but now she looks even smaller. The bed is a double and yet she is swimming in it. The sight makes Paul tearful, but he hides this from Louise. His crying always makes her cry.

Paul has never been at the side of anyone's deathbed before. Even the word *deathbed* makes him shiver. He pulls out his phone to see if there's a Cree word for it, something more elegant, but there isn't.

"Oh, Paul," Louise says. She extends her hand. Paul inches closer and grabs it. "You look thin," she says. He laughs. She's always wanted him to be a bit chubby because to her it meant he'd been eating well. She was adamant he never went hungry as a kid.

"Tell me, how's Julia. Is she here?" Louise scans the room.

"She's in Edmonton, Mom. She had to work."

"Always working, that one. And you? Why aren't you working?"

"I took time off."

"Not because of me, I hope."

"Of course I did!"

Louise shakes her head. "Well, thank you."

She lets out a few labored coughs, and the sound upsets Paul.

"Who were your visitors?"

"Just some of the old ones." "Old ones" is what Louise calls the elders. She excludes herself from that category, despite belonging to it. Paul can't remember how old she is—75? 80? When did he stop keeping count?

"And what did you talk about?"

"My parents, I wanted to be sure I was remembering them as best I could."

Paul is moved. On her deathbed, Louise is once again a daughter.

"Tell me about them," he says.

Louise considers this. Paul feels silly. "I'm exhausted, my boy. I think I'll shut my eyes for a bit."

"OK, Mom, I'll be here."

Louise falls asleep almost immediately. Paul retrieves his suitcase from the SUV and puts it in his childhood bedroom, which has changed very little since he left decades ago. He didn't have much in it growing up—a bed, a dresser, his clothes, some toys. He has never needed much to be content, which was likely a result of Louise's maternal attention.

He returns to the living room and watches Louise sleep. It occurs to him that he has seldom spent time looking at his mother, deliberately taking in her physical form. In his mind she suffered from the condition of omnipresence. She faded into his psychic backdrop, where everything is either blurry or terribly clear. He was afraid to look at her long enough to find himself laid bare in her features and demeanor. He wanted so feverishly to be different; it was an adolescent rebellion that lingered longer than it deserved to. Decades later, she has now become incandescent to him, like a sudden burst of light. All light, alas, exists only in the past tense. It has always already fallen.

As he watches Louise, he thinks about the first time he brought Julia to the reserve to meet her, shortly after they began dating. They had both started new jobs, on break for some holiday, Paul can't recall which. Julia was very charismatic; an air of authority surrounded her, and she commanded social attention. Louise wanted to take care of her nonetheless, but Julia resisted, not wanting to be a burden. That evening Paul was whisked away by some cousins, so Louise and Julia kept each other company. When he returned, Louise pulled him aside to say, "She's not really one of us." Paul looked at her quizzically.

"Not from the rez," she clarified. "She isn't like us."

Paul was offended on Julia's behalf and suspected the comment was meant to elicit shame in him too—all the time he'd spent in the city. He knew, though, that the reserve did lodge itself inside those who lived there; its history courses inside him still. All people from the reserve bear at least a trace of its origins as an open-air prison. Certain norms and behaviors emerged over time, both as coping mechanisms and as subversive remakings of everyday life. People sculpted and continue to sculpt reserve life, but it is also true that the reserve sculpts them. In Louise's mind, Paul and Julia would always be at a distance from each other, even if that distance was quite small to others. Louise believed it was big enough to engulf them both; love didn't always have to mean a spectacle of difference. What wounded Paul most was that Louise saw a trace of this otherness in him too. It was her way of saying, *You're becoming someone else, someone I barely know.*

. . .

WHEN LOUISE RECEIVED THE DIAGNOSIS, she didn't call Paul for a week. She didn't know how to tell him. Plus, at that point, they only talked every other week—she wanted to wait to maintain their normal rhythm of correspondence. What's more, her idea of what kind of person he was had by that point become quite vague. She wasn't able to anticipate or decipher his emotions—a skill that should come naturally to a mother—until he explicitly expressed them himself. She spent days hesitating, holding on to the news, afraid of what it would do to him, and then to her. When she finally called him, Paul broke down after they hung up. The delay seemed cruel, because it meant he'd have even fewer days with her. He drove up that night, arriving after midnight. Louise had long been asleep, but she left the door unlocked. The next day, they cried in the same room for the first time since his father's funeral. Julia arrived the next morning but had to leave that night. Paul can barely place her in the memory, as if she hadn't been there at all.

· · ·

IN THE EVENING, Louise wakens. Paul is still on the couch, facing her.

"You haven't been there this whole time, have you?" she asks playfully.

"Are you hungry?"

"Oh, I don't eat a whole lot these days."

"Oh god, of course. I'm sorry." Paul keeps forgetting how severe her illness is despite visual proof of Louise's shrinking body.

"I've been meaning to ask." Louise pauses. "Will you keep the house?"

Paul looks around at the humble structure, built by her father. Somehow, he hadn't considered the possibility that he'd inherit it.

"You get everything, Paul," she says.

This dismays him. Is there really no one else to be included in her will? What will he do with it all?

"I don't want to think about it, Mom."

"You have to," she says. The short sentence seems to tire her.

Paul stands up and looks out the window, where a young man he doesn't recognize is walking purposefully along the edge of the road. It feels like proof of how alien he's become to the reserve.

"I don't know that it's that simple, Mom."

"No, it is," she says.

THE NEXT MORNING, a nurse arrives to attend to Louise. She administers her medication, then readies her for a bath, during which Paul steps out for air. He gets in his vehicle and drives down an unmaintained road until he reaches the lake. The path to the water is wet and muddy. He trudges on and cries gently when he gets to the shore. Mosquitoes swarm him. Paul thinks about his job and how he once aspired to start his own consultancy firm. That dream now feels less urgent, even silly. He should work less, he thinks. He should tell Julia he wants to relocate to the reserve, to live with her in his childhood home, or he will live in it without her (though he'd much prefer the former). It's impulsive, but he doesn't care; the desire hums inside him. He has just enough service to call Julia, even though she's working. She doesn't answer, so he leaves a voicemail.

Hey dear, don't be alarmed. Nothing's wrong, relatively speaking. I'm sure you're at work. Hope things aren't too overwhelming. I saw the article about the crowded emergency rooms. Please take a break, drink some water when you can. I just wanted to say that I miss you and that I love you. OK, talk later. Bye now.

PAUL SIFTS THROUGH LOUISE'S BELONGINGS while she sleeps. He's in the basement, a place he feared as a kid but now finds himself feeling emotionally drawn to even though it's still dim and dank and crawling with spiders. In a box, he finds regalia. He pulls out a fancy shawl that has Louise's name embroidered on a tag on an inseam. He didn't know she danced before he was born. He's sad he doesn't have a daughter to pass the regalia on to. Louise would've loved that. She would've been an amazing kokum, he thinks. His childlessness feels like another way he disappointed her. It's another thing he feels remorse over. He wishes he could've made her at least marginally happier. Children are terrible at accounting for the happiness of their parents. Knowing this doesn't make Paul feel any better.

. . .

LOUISE UNDERWENT A ROUND OF CHEMOTHERAPY, but the cancer was already aggressive. The doctor explained that the treatment would only delay the inevitable. Louise prayed that the cancer would retreat anyways. She added traditional Cree medicine to her regimen, various tinctures and teas. At first, her condition seemed to improve, but then the cancer spread to yet another organ. Louise didn't discuss the specifics of her health or treatment plan with Paul. When he asked, she changed the subject. All he knew was that the chemo was more than her body could handle.

It was suggested that Louise spend her last days in hospice, to be sure she was adequately attended to. But she wanted to stay at her house as long as possible; it seemed obvious to draw her life to a close there, a place she had lived in across two centuries. Paul knew that to attempt to convince her otherwise would be futile. She's tenacious, like the Cree women who came before her. It's one of the qualities he has admired most in her.

≡

AFTER A WEEK ON THE RESERVE, Paul settles into a pattern: he builds his day around Louise's naps. When she sleeps, he reads, checks emails, texts Julia. Sometimes he walks, but not far. Today, relatives have come to spend time with Louise. There are about fifteen people in the house, which doesn't quite accommodate everyone. There's a lot of laughter, some tears. One of Louise's cousins tells a story about the day Louise gave birth to Paul. Apparently, they had to travel through a blizzard to get to the hospital. The ambulance hadn't made it in time and it met them halfway to the hospital. She gave birth to him in the ambulance; they called him a miracle baby. Somehow, it's the first time Paul has heard the story. What other facts about himself, he wonders, does he not know? And is it already too late to find out? To himself, he acknowledges that part of him, unknown and mythical, will disappear when Louise passes.

In the evening, Paul helps prepare a large meal. He tends to the stew, because the women don't trust him with anything else. This is fine by him. He hasn't been in a room with so many of his relatives in decades. He tries to enjoy the occasion, but he doesn't know how to. His grief is too enormous, as pervasive as the past.

Louise smiles as everyone eats, but then she becomes sick. Paul carries her to the bathroom to vomit—there are too many people in the house to use the wheelchair. The relatives all pause conversation to watch him cradle his mother in his arms like a child. The sight of it distorts time. No one speaks for several minutes. The sound of Louise's vomiting is too difficult to bear, so people begin to tidy up, parting ways silently. Someone knocks at the door, but Paul is seated on the bathroom floor beside Louise, rubbing her back. She continues to grip the toilet.

ONCE EVERYONE HAS LEFT and Louise is back in bed, Paul works on a crossword in a newspaper someone left behind.

"Paul?"

Her voice surprises him; he thought she was asleep.

"Yes, Mom?"

"Do you have any regrets?"

"In life?"

"Yes."

Paul ponders. "Maybe I should've had a kid, been a better husband, come home more often . . . invested more." It all feels trivial.

Louise considers his answer. "I think you're a good husband. Your dad was." Paul knows he hasn't been as good of a husband as his dad was to Louise, but he doesn't push the topic any further.

"What about you, Mom?"

"What?"

"Regrets?"

"Oh, right." She pauses. "I've lived a good life. Regrets don't mean anything to me anymore. The living get to have regrets. You still get to change your life." Paul sits up straighter. "If you want to have a kid, then do it. If you don't love Julia anymore, then don't drag her along because you're scared. If you want more money—well, maybe that one isn't as important. I never had much money in my life. I never needed it."

"I'm not ready to lose you." Paul's eyes water. He can't see anything, except for Louise's blurry outline.

"I know, my boy." Her voice is steady. "You don't need to be." She watches him wipe his eyes. "I hope heaven really does exist," she says. Paul glances over at the portrait of Jesus above her, which is crooked. "I hope your dad is waiting for me." She shuts her eyes.

Paul walks over and kisses her forehead. He hasn't kissed her since childhood. He does regret this.

Louise opens her eyes.

"I hope heaven looks like the rez," she says.

Paul laughs, but he's also crying.

"I hope it's autumn all the time."

She holds Paul's face in her hand. He thinks about how much more living he has to do—a cruelty. He wonders what the world will be without her in it. The truth: it will be nothing and it will be everything.

Louise musters what strength she has left to rest her forehead against his.

Time doesn't so much pass as fill the room up, like snow.

NOTES AND ACKNOWLEDGMENTS

Works cited include "One Art" by Elizabeth Bishop, "Visual Pleasure and Narrative Cinema" by Laura Mulvey, "Landscape" by Louise Glück, *Ghostly Matters* by Avery Gordon, and *To the Lighthouse* by Virginia Woolf.

The line "To paint the world is to believe in it" in "Lived Experience" is a remix of poet Richard Siken's line "If you don't believe in the world it would be / stupid to paint it" from *War of the Foxes*.

Shout out to Emily Riddle with whom I've had conversations about chaotic Indigenous love, which influenced some of the thinking in "Lived Experience."

The Yoko Ono nod in "Poetry Class" is a reference to *Grapefruit*. The Audre Lorde nod is a reference to "Poetry Is not a Luxury."

The information on trembling poplars mentioned in "Various People" can be found here: https://www.awes-ab.ca/species /trembling-aspen/.

≡

Thank you, Cody, my agent. Thank you, David and Mo, my editors. It's a true joy to work with you all.

Thank you, *Maisonneuve*, for publishing an early version of "One Woman's Memories."